The World of Nagaraj

R. K. Narayan's writing spans the greatest period of change in modern Indian history, from the days of the Raj – *Swami and Friends* (1935), *The Bachelor of Arts* (1937) and *The English Teacher* (1945) – to recent years of political unrest – *The Painter of Signs* (1976), *A Tiger for Malgudi* (1983), *Talkative Man* (1987). He has published numerous collections of short stories, including *Malgudi Days* (1982) and *Under the Banyan Tree* (1985) and several works of non-fiction. His most recent work is *The Grandmother's Tale – Three Novellas*, published by William Heinemann in 1993.

Also by R. K. Narayan

NOVELS OF MALGUDI
*The Bachelor of Arts
*The Dark Room
*The English Teacher
*The Financial Expert
The Guide
The Man-Eater of Malgudi
*Mr Sampath – The Printer of Malgudi
*Swami and Friends
The Vendor of Sweets
The Painter of Signs
A Tiger for Malgudi
*Waiting for the Mahatma

****

*Gods, Demons and Others
The Ramayana
The Mahabharata

STORIES
*The Grandmother's Tale: Three Novellas
A Horse and Two Goats
An Astrologer's Day and Other Stories
Lawley Road
Malgudi Days
Under the Banyan Tree and Other Stories

MEMOIRS
My Days

TRAVEL
My Dateless Diary
The Emerald Route

ESSAYS
Next Saturday
Reluctant Guru

**available from Minerva*

R. K. NARAYAN

The World of Nagaraj

Minerva

A Minerva Paperback
THE WORLD OF NAGARAJ

First published in Great Britain 1990
by William Heinemann Ltd
This Minerva edition published 1994
by Mandarin Paperbacks
an imprint of Reed Consumer Books Ltd
Michelin House, 81 Fulham Road, London SW3 6RB
and Auckland, Melbourne, Singapore and Toronto

A CIP catalogue record for this title
is available from the British Library
ISBN 0 7493 9744 6

Printed and bound in Great Britain
by Cox & Wyman Ltd, Reading, Berks

To Ram and Susan,
whose involvement with Nagaraj
at every stage, since inception,
helped me no end.

CHAPTER I

Nagaraj fancied himself a man with a mission. If you asked, 'What is your mission?' he would look away and pretend not to have heard your query. He was not quite clear in his mind about his mission, but always felt he must be up and doing. He could not stay in bed after the hall clock struck six, but his wife, who got up first, would say, 'Where is the hurry? Why don't you sleep till seven as others do? None of them to be seen so early except your good self . . .' and, rising, hurry off to the back yard to start her day with a cold bath and the washing of clothes. Nagaraj would stay in bed till all sound from the back yard ceased, when he could be sure she had moved into the kitchen to light the fire and put the coffee kettle on or had entered the puja room to mutter a prayer before the gods. Now it was certain she would not cross his path and accost him with, 'Why should you get up so early?' Not in his nature to retort openly, though he would probably mumble within himself, 'Just my wish, and that's that.' He would get up and pass along briskly to the back yard for a wash.

After his morning coffee, he stepped out and strolled along to wake up his friend Jayaraj, the photographer, who slept on a bench in front of his shop at the market archway. Nagaraj sat on the edge of the bench while Jayaraj was still asleep and glanced through a one-sheet morning paper, which Truth Printing published, giving a summary of news items culled from yesterday's papers and radio broadcasts. It cost ten paise a day and, though Jayaraj paid the subscription, the first to read it was Nagaraj, who always arrived with the delivery boy. Nagaraj read through it in four minutes and picked up talking points for the day. 'The minister is going to Bermuda,' Nagaraj would announce to Jayaraj when he opened his eyes.

'Which minister?'

'One of them, there are so many . . .'

'What for?'

'I don't know. How can I guess? No explanation. I must speak to the printer. Only one sheet for ten paise and one side filled with advertisements!'

'What sort of advertisement? Just rubbish. What have we in this town? Manufacturers? Any notable enterprises? Any personality of importance? Nothing to advertise.'

'Not so bad. I wouldn't agree with you,' said Nagaraj. 'We have our own shops and men, our town can grow and develop gradually if a vision is kept up before the public through advertisements. Above all, this paper gives us an idea of what is going on around us, also of shops, marriages, vacant houses, deaths . . .'

'All packed on one side of a sheet!' Jayaraj sneered. 'I'd stop it if the Truth Printing man was not my friend desperately needing support.'

'I don't mind it. Such frugal fare saves us time, and some tit-bits and information are useful for my work . . .'

Jayaraj ignored Nagaraj's mention of work, stood up and said, 'Now wait here, I will dash across to my house for a wash, and come back. I don't want to leave the place unguarded, demons are around ready to break the lock . . .' He indicated the inside of the shop and said, 'Irreplaceable treasures there. Everyone, every blackguard who passes through this market gate has an eye on my camera and equipment.'

'But why do you always borrow the Trustee's imported camera?'

'That's for outdoor purpose only, but the one in there is my own, the best lens. Whether you aim it at a corpse or a bridegroom, it's all the same to it. Have you ever considered how impartial the lens could be?'

'Ah, ah! How profound your thoughts . . .'

'Very few appreciate me; they think I'm just a common photographer, little realising that the man behind a camera must be a thinker, otherwise he will end up as a lens-wiper.'

'True, true, that's what I want to emphasise in my book too.'

Jayaraj checked himself from enquiring about the book. Otherwise he would have to sit there and listen to Nagaraj's grandiloquent plan to write on Sage Narada. The first time Nagaraj had mentioned the subject, Jayaraj had blundered into asking 'Why Narada?', thereby starting Nagaraj on the celestial sage who had a curse on his back that unless he spread a gossip a day his head would burst. The sage floated along with ease from one world to another among the fourteen worlds above and below this earth, carrying news and gossip, often causing clashes between gods and demons, demons and demons, and gods and gods, and between creatures of the earth. Ultimately, of course, such clashes and destruction proved beneficial in a cosmic perspective. Evil destroyed itself. That was Nagaraj's thesis. Jayaraj realised that he often ignored a customer as he was engrossed in Nagaraj's talk, and in course of time became wary whenever Nagaraj showed symptoms of leading on to the subject of his book. He got up and left but was soon back to open his shop.

Nagaraj left his post and ambled along to watch the stalls. The shutters were just going up, the shopmen heaping vegetables and fruits on shelves and on the floor. Nagaraj derived a strange pleasure from looking at the exhibit of farm produce: 'That mound of cabbages looks beautiful,' he reflected as he walked down the narrow space between the stalls. 'Also those brinjals shining green and purple – all these are attractive, like flowers in a garden – but what a pity they are cut up and cooked – when served on the plate, how different, greasy and mangled they seem! Can't say it to my wife, she will take it as a comment on her cooking . . . Have to be careful and diplomatic all the time, the tightrope walking called domestic harmony. Nowadays she is too ready to take offence.' His was a familiar figure in the market. He was hailed here and there as he passed, but he preferred not to do any marketing today. He replied, 'Not today, I have no money now . . .'

'Not at all necessary. I can take it later. You are like our bank . . .' But he kept moving, laughing at the joke, secretly worrying whether he should not stop and carry that bitter gourd which looks like, like what? He fumbled for a comparison and gave it up. Later it occurred to him that the bitter gourd was patterned after a minor crocodile with hieroglyphics on its back. He marvelled for a second at nature's variety. 'No two vegetables alike,' he commented to himself, 'some of them even more grotesque than the bitter gourd. Nature's jokes!'

He walked home, the back of his mind worrying over something. He wished he could define the worry and exorcise it. He found he had nothing to worry about. 'Thank God I don't have to think of money. I'm not greedy, that's why I'm happy. Even after the division of property, I get a thousand rupees from the bank deposits left by my father. Fortunately he specified my share, otherwise it would have been bitter arguments with my brother, who showed a fighting temperament while asking for his share of the property after Father's death. But of that let me not think now; I had enough at that time. Never wish to think of it. If I want more money I could rent out a portion of my house: with the pressure on housing at present, anyone will be happy to give me at least three hundred for a portion and the property is big enough for both parties to co-exist without coming in each other's way. But is it worth it? No,' he told himself. 'My old mother should have her freedom to hobble up and down unrestricted, and my wife must have her freedom to talk, comment, argue and shout uninhibited, without any tenant watching – after all, it is her privilege and I do not have to listen to her full speech; I can move away to the pyol.'

When he reached home he didn't knock on the door but divested his feet of the sandals at the doorway and, hoisting himself on the smooth cool pyol, sat down leaning against the pillar on the verandah. He loved its cool granite surface and could now watch the goings-on in Kabir Street.

For the next hour or two he would not stir out of his perch. When he sat thus, he was filled with a sense of supreme contentment, never wanting anything more out of life. The activities of his neighbours fascinated him. He could enumerate the timing of every arrival and departure.

The Talkative Man should be out in fifteen minutes. His was the first house in the row. He was the busiest man in the street, fancied himself a journalist and wandered about the town the whole day on his bicycle. Nagaraj wondered what he got out of it. 'None of my business, I suppose. His forefathers have left him the big house and enough money to keep him going. Blessed fellow, never married, unlike me, a prisoner of domesticity. Oh, no! I should not be saying such things – rather unfair and insulting to the poor creature my wife, who has not had a day's rest, serving me and my mother ungrudgingly, though she has moments of nerves when she would flare up at me or my mother, especially my mother, but that'll always pass . . .'

His thoughts turned to Sambu, his immediate neighbour, hardly to be seen outside, a contrast to the Talkative Man. Sambu sat glued to a canvas deck chair beside the street window, reading a book all day as long as the light lasted, and at dusk he switched on a reading lamp and continued. 'What a lot he reads, unsocial fellow: never shows any interest in anyone but just goes on reading; anyway what is there to read all the time, poor fellow, bound to grow flabby and shapeless if he goes on like that. Decent fellow, never interferes with anyone but just goes on reading. Why should I mind? It's his business; only I want him to remain in good shape. He has put on weight after his mother's death. He must at least go for an early morning walk along the river. Lazy fellow. His father was a skinflint moneylender who confiscated a whole library which a poor scholar had built up laboriously, although his monthly budget remained unbalanced all his life. On his death, Sambu's father attached the library along with the rosewood shelves through a court order, and Sambu has done nothing but read all day, after his father's death. Rather unhealthy for the eyes. They should pass a law that one should read only books personally acquired or earned, not an inheritance.'

There was a slight noise at the door on the other side. He knew that his mother was trying to open the door but he knew also that she could not move it. It was massive, of ancient teakwood, tanned through time and weather, the framework with lotus-like carvings, brass knobs on the central panel shaped like virginal breasts, so shining and attractive that, when very young, Nagaraj used to stand on his toes and try to reach those nipples with his lips; his brother, who was taller and always luckier, took his mouth to the knobs and clicked his tongue in appreciation, crying, 'Oh, that milk is so sweet,' and made Nagaraj envious. They also played trains standing on the bottom ledge of the door and clutching the brass knobs to push and pull the door.

'Nagu! Nagu!' his mother cried from the other side. 'The water is getting cold, come for your bath.'

'She still thinks I am ten years old, doesn't notice my age – that I'm past fifty.' She was frail and wasp-like, and hobbled about the house with a staff in hand.

'Nagu, Nagu,' her thin voice plaintively continued on the other side of the door. He understood his wife's strategy. If she had come out to call him, he would have snapped back (he imagined), 'Don't disturb me now.' But Mother's intrusion was different. He stirred himself and said mildly, 'I know when to bathe, Mother.' He knew he sounded pompous, while he had only been watching and wool-gathering, which were important activities in his scheme of living. Watching and brooding had a subtle value which people never realised. Left to himself he was prepared to sit on the pyol the whole day, looking on the life and movement of Kabir Street. Now he could not ignore his mother's call. 'How old is she? Must be seventy or eighty or ninety – lost count of her years, as it was the family tradition generally not to celebrate anyone's birthday beyond the tenth. "Happy Birthday" greetings were a western fashion,' he thought. At once he corrected himself. 'What about the elaborate ritual on one's sixtieth year?' His brother, he remembered, had celebrated two months ago his sixtieth birthday like a wedding, with printed invitation and pipe and drum and garland and feast at his village home, having himself and his wife photographed in bridal costume. (Jayaraj was a special invitee.) It was a grand occasion in the village and he had to attend it, leaving his mother behind in the care of the woman who came in daily to sweep the house and was now cajoled into staying all day with a bonus of ten rupees. Mother was delighted because she liked the woman, who had been in their service for years out of count and was a dependable ally against the daughter-in-law. His brother's sixtieth birthday was memorable. He had entertained the entire village, hundreds of guests for each meal – they had spread dining leaves in every corner of their home and also outside on the street, blocking all passage for the day. Nagaraj felt a little awkward about it as he noticed his brother and sister-in-law going through elaborate ceremonies conducted by showy priests from Trichy and then moving around, giggling like newly-weds, with garlands dangling from their necks. Jayaraj had managed to borrow the imported camera from the Trustee and was in his element, clicking away. A lot of village men surrounded him and ventured to ask to be photographed.

He said, 'Certainly, five rupees a copy and you must come to town to collect it.'

His brother, who overheard it, was in such a jolly mood

– unknown in normal days – that he said, 'Jayaraj, take their photos also. I'll pay.'

Nagaraj responded to his brother's good mood by sticking to him all through and laughing at his banal jokes unreservedly. He had brought presents for the occasion, brocades and silks for his sister-in-law from Coomar's and a pair of dhotis, lace-edged two inches, for his brother, and silverware and a wristwatch for his nephew Tim. Nagaraj's wife was very solicitous and tried to please her sister-in-law in a hundred ways while she, in turn, pressed sweets, coffee and drinks on her in-laws from the town. They were laughing, joking and smiling at one another endlessly, and sang songs sitting before the holy fire. 'What makes them so happy on a birthday? I'd feel gloomy if I realised I was sixty. Birthdays must be ignored, as occasions, taking one inescapably a step nearer decrepitude and decay!' One must be as innocent as the old watchman at the temple who had to sign a form – with his thumb impression – and declare his age for a pension now and then. He always begged Nagaraj to fill in the columns. It was no use asking his age since he always said, 'I don't know, sir. We poor people are not taught to count. You have wisdom and must know how old I am by looking at me.'

Nagaraj would study his lined face and the bent back and declare, 'Seventy-seven. Next year remember to say seventy-eight and not twenty-four.'

He heard his mother's call again and rose, switching off his reveries. When he pushed the door open she was there like a hovering spirit. He felt annoyed at her persistence and wanted to shout, 'Why don't you leave me alone?' but sublimated his words, 'Yes, yes, it won't take more than five minutes. I'll be ready.' What would be the point in losing his temper? Apart from other considerations she was deaf and never understood a word.

His wife was in the second courtyard and glared at him speechlessly as he passed. 'Why is she scowling? I've done nothing . . . It's becoming difficult to survive in the company of these two women,' he reflected, compressing his lips, sealing his remarks which might rush forth to say, 'If you have no one to heckle, don't choose me.' His wife just said, 'If the water gets cold, I can't light the fire again.'

He took his bath in the back yard, behind the screen of a couple of zinc sheets. Bathrooms were a recent notion; they were unknown earlier. They had always washed and bathed in the river which flowed along the back of their Kabir Street homes. When the chill wind blew from the river they set up a cauldron on a pile of bricks under the mango tree and heated the water with brambles and twigs from the back yard wilderness.

Now the water was the right temperature. His wife had a genius for doing the right thing and he felt a profound gratitude for her attention as he poured water over his head and messed about with the green soap, which as usual smarted at his eyes. 'She has a purpose in hustling me to bathe; otherwise one has to go about collecting faggots again. But should not the matter be left to my good sense too? Can't I judge what I should do in consideration of everyone's welfare? It's not Mother and my wife alone who are concerned. I'm the head of the family. Let no one forget it . . .' At this point he tried to switch off his mind again – too much of thinking is no good, rather fatiguing.

The bath was refreshing and, as always, induced in him a holy mood. After a bath he always picked up an ochre drape and dhoti suspended from a nail at the door of the puja room. He had acquired them a few months ago after a laborious search. One day he found a bearded sadhu at the Town Hall on the lawn, who wore the ochre robe of a holy man. Nagaraj approached him timidly, the other's appearance being overwhelming, and asked with humility, 'Where can I get cloth similar to yours?'

The sadhu looked at Nagaraj fixedly. 'Why?'

Nagaraj felt confused and said, 'I like it.'

'That is not a good enough reason. This raiment is sacred and meant for one who is a sanyasi. Are you one or do you want to be one?'

Nagaraj felt embarrassed and tongue-tied. 'I've a family . . .'

'How large?'

'I've an old mother and wife.'

'No children?'

Nagaraj shook his head and said, 'But my brother in the village has a son.'

'How does that help you?'

Nagaraj now felt emboldened to sit beside the sadhu on the soft lawn, the only green spot in the town. For some reason or the other the Municipality maintained with care this green patch. Nagaraj said further, 'But I'm fond of my brother's son, Tim . . .'

'Tim! Who gave him such a name? What does it mean?'

Nagaraj felt caught. He had no explanation.

'Every god in Heaven has a thousand names – couldn't you pick up one of them instead of Tim? What does it mean, anyway?'

'When he was a year old the only noise he could lisp was "Tim". It was charming and everyone began to address him as Tim – though his actual name at the naming ceremony was Krishnaji.'

'Ah! Highest God, and you have chosen to call him Tim, which should be the name of only a wandering cat!'

'Such things somehow happen, Swamiji. No one can be responsible for such mistakes. But in all school registers his name is Krishnaji.'

'Do you know why we name children after the gods? So that His name in some form is always on one's lips and the walls echo divine names!'

'Ah! What profound words!' Nagaraj cried.

The sanyasi was flattered and commanded, 'State your business with us.'

'Just wanted to know how I can acquire those ochre robes . . .'

The sanyasi looked down at his chest and said, 'These days people have a craving for fancy clothes.' He swept around his arm to indicate the crowds on the lawn. 'Do you see anyone who is not dressed like a clown in all this crowd?'

'All kinds of flowery patterns and colours! Sometimes I feel those men wear women's saris instead of dhotis. You can't find a white dhoti anywhere – all in fancy clothes as your good self remarked a little while ago . . .' echoed Nagaraj.

The sanyasi laughed, pleased at the concurrence. Nagaraj felt inspired to continue, 'Did you notice the youth of the country? – in tight pants and jeans and T-shirts and, as I hear it, schoolgirls crop their hair and wear short skirts while boys wear long uncut hair. You must forgive my mentioning these things . . .' He knew he was exaggerating these fashions which were more noticeable in a city like Madras than in Malgudi and actually were known in Malgudi only through photographs in magazines, but it pleased the sanyasi to hear such sweeping statements in support of his own observation and he came back to the question of the ochre robe. 'Now, explain why you want to dress like a sanyasi. There are enough fakes in holy men's garb.'

Nagaraj explained, 'I thought it would give me greater peace of mind at home if I wore a sanyasi's dress in the puja room, at least . . .'

Nagaraj met the sanyasi again at the same place two days later. The sanyasi handed him a packet. 'This is ochre dye. Dissolve it in water and soak your clothes in it overnight, and there in the morning you will be ready to look like a sage.'

'I don't want to parade it, but wear it only when I perform a puja.'

'Wear it for an hour or a lifetime, I don't care what you do, but only remember when you are wearing this ochre your mind should be only on God, not on money or the family. Your thoughts must be away from all sensual matters, free from kama, krodha, lobha and moha. You must observe silence, become deaf to other people's voices, never pay attention to it, even if there is an urgent telegram – '

'No one sends me a telegram.'

'Don't interrupt, but listen. Never hear the knock on the door. Don't look at your wife except as a mother, and don't let your mind dwell on your night life – '

'I have none now. For over ten years we have been living like brother and sister.'

'Don't interrupt,' commanded the sanyasi, and Nagaraj was happy to shut up. Even as he was explaining his private life he was not sure he was truthful: he remembered that some nights, in the darkness, at a deep silent hour, he slipped down from his cot and sought his wife's body while she slept on a mattress on the floor. 'Even that must be given up,' he told himself. 'No more . . .'

After his bath he took the ochre dhoti and the wrap and briskly dried himself with it as he entered the puja room, a cubicle at a corner off the second courtyard, which for generations had been the family prayer room. His wife had already lit the oil lamps before the deity, filled a basket with flowers from the garden in the back yard, and lit incense sticks. Now in his ochre robe he felt transformed. While he was in this dress, his wife was not to bring up any domestic matter or any letter in the post, never call him to the street door, even if an emperor knocked. She had to conduct herself as if he had ceased to exist. His mind worked further on the theme. It was a state of being dead for some moments each day. His guru, the Town Hall sanyasi, had explained, 'It's good to experience death a little each day so that when your time is up you will slip into the state effortlessly. You will realise how noble and welcome it is – then Death will not be dreaded and avoided. You will overcome death itself . . .' Nagaraj sat in his cubicle before the brass images lit up by the flickering oil lamps, and felt elevated. He recited in an undertone fragments of vedic hymns he had learnt and half forgotten, all the holy verse he knew and the mantras he was taught in boyhood. He showered flowers on the images. The fragrance of incense and flowers gave him a feeling of sitting in a haven of peace, silence, isolation. He felt he had been vouched a rare guidance by the sanyasi. The first time he wore the sanyasi's garb, his wife withdrew into the kitchen and shut the door with a bang. She was sullen. He wanted to assure her that the garb and restrictions were to last only for thirty minutes, but he had no way of communicating the message as he had to observe silence when he was dressed thus. He swallowed back his words and stepped into the puja room.

When he finished his puja and came out and changed into normal white dress, he asked, 'Why have you shut yourself in?'

'So that your meditation may not be spoilt by the sound of my breathing.'

'The kitchen smoke might affect your eyes,' Nagaraj said.

'Ah! How considerate! So much the better if I'm not able to watch your antics. Anyway, why are you doing these funny things?' He wondered how to explain and if he could tell her the need for a short course of daily death as a rehearsal for the final one. He checked himself as he realised that she might not understand the philosophy but feel shocked and lament at the mention of death and bring the neighbours gate-crashing. And so he hummed and hawed and blinked till she said, 'You don't know the reason yourself! Some fool has put it in your head . . .'

'Oh, no, don't call him a fool,' he pleaded.

'Whom? Who is he?'

He did not wish to betray the source of his inspiration and mumbled inconsequentially.

Eventually she got used to the change, realising it was harmless and that the ochre robe would be on for only thirty minutes.

When he emerged from the special garb and dressed normally in a white dhoti and banian, she would say, 'Your food is ready.' He followed her and sat down on a wooden plank at his usual place under the window. His oval silver plate would be set down and food served on it. He would eat with relish and feel like expressing some appreciation: 'I'd never have thought that salted cucumber would be so good. Should I fetch some more from the market tomorrow?'

She felt relieved and said, 'Don't bother. The woman who brings a basket offers a good selection – all her vegetables are fresh . . .'

'She gets them probably from the farms direct, while in the market they are carried in lorries from wholesale traders – you must come with me to the market to look at the mounds of fresh cabbage, a great spectacle, I tell you – '

'How can I come? Who will be with Mother? She is restless, moving all the time, and if she has a fall while no one is here – God help us . . .'

'You fear the worst. We could tell her to be careful and not to bolt the door while we are out . . .' He realised he was getting into unnecessary detail.

His wife said, 'No need to talk of all that now.' Her secret grievance was that his mother had become her sole concern while Nagaraj went about freely without a care. She often said, when the mood was dark, that she had become a prisoner in the house owing to the old lady's restlessness. He thought it best not to pursue the subject. He terminated the theme then and there and, after uttering a few pleasantries, rose and walked to the backyard to wash his fingers and gargle. He was so satisfied with the meal he had consumed that he felt like uttering a compliment to please his wife. His mind buzzed with ideas but he was hesitant since he had to weigh his words to avoid complicated discussions about Mother once again. He just said, 'Some new patterns seem to have arrived at the Sari Centre. We must make some special arrangement so that you may have a look at them . . .' His wife did not reply; she realised that he was being pleasant without commitment and ignored his offer. Unless they engaged some nurse to guard his mother, it would be impossible to leave home. Even her evening visits to the nearby temple had to be manoeuvred. She had to seek a neighbour's help and get back in a dashing hurry. That always left a feeling that she did not give the god at the temple enough time.

After eating, Nagaraj did not stay in. He dressed briskly before a long mirror hanging by a nail in his room, a family heirloom which reflected one's figure chin down to knee if one stood straight in front of it and the other areas if one stooped. He was satisfied with his looks, his dress and deportment. He wore for his outings a special kind of snow-white dhoti with gold thread on the edge, a blue shirt and an upper cloth also white. He was satisfied that his personality was impressive enough.

His routine first stop was Kanni's stall at the market corner – an old chum of his primary-school days at the municipal free school in Vinayak Street. It was a one-room building with discoloured tiles on its roof. All classes were held in the same hall with four teachers in four corners bawling out their lessons over the children's babble and wielding their canes freely, whacking, as a matter of policy, the nearest child. Nagaraj's father found it practical to send his two children here: it was close by and the children could go up without escort, and it was also cheap, being a municipal school, no fee, except an occasional cash present to the teacher. Nagaraj used to sit on the same bench as Kanni and they were whacked together by their teacher. His brother sat away on a different bench, being in a senior class in that hall. He maintained himself aloof as a superior person and never encouraged Nagaraj to walk beside him to school, preferring the company of boys of the same height. If, by chance, Nagaraj got mixed in his company he ordered him off. Luckily, very soon he demanded to be sent to the Board High School in another direction, and Nagaraj felt happy to be free from his company. But Kanni stuck to him and instead of going home after the classes they played marbles in the street until Nagaraj's father came out to drag him home. Eventually they pursued different careers. Nagaraj went to the Albert Mission School and Kanni became an apprentice under his father, who was a carpenter.

Later he built a bunk at the market corner and opened a little shop selling cigarettes, soda, and betel leaves and tobacco for chewing. It was a strategic corner and attracted a crowd while Kanni himself, now middle-aged, sat on a low stool inside the shop and served the customers crowding in front.

Nagaraj stopped and Kanni greeted him with, 'What's the news?'

'Nothing much. Floods, droughts, fights and speeches by ministers.'

'Is that all?'

'The minister has left for Bermuda to market our handloom cloth – '

'Which minister?'

'I don't know. I can only repeat the newspaper.'

'Where is Bermuda?' Kanni asked mechanically, holding out a small aluminium spoonful of arecanut and four tender betel leaves smeared with lime. Nagaraj rolled them up with arecanut and stuffed them into his mouth and enjoyed the slight tingling sensation it produced. Little beads of perspiration broke out on his brow and he said, 'Put it on my account, as usual . . .'

'Of course. Even in my dream I can remember who owes me how much.'

'Any time you want the account settled . . .' said Nagaraj, chewing the pan, lips red with betel juice. You could not find a more contented soul in Malgudi at that moment. In that mood he passed on to his next station. Half a mile along the market road, turning left he got into Grove Street, a mainly residential area, and passed under an arch over a gate announcing in grand style: COOMAR'S BOEING SARI CENTRE. Raman, the sign-board painter, was offered a special fee to make the lettering impressive. It hit the eye the moment you turned the corner.

Earlier in their life, Coomar (a self-made man) had struck a lasting friendship with Nagaraj at the Boardless Coffee House, where they generally met when Nagaraj was studying at the Albert Mission College. Those days, Nagaraj avoided going home when his classes were over for the day. Evening was a dull hour at home with his father poring over accounts or discussing agricultural matters with visitors from the village and his mother was away at the temple listening to a religious discourse, and his brother was in his room chatting with a friend. Nagaraj shared the room with him but was forbidden to enter it when he had friends there. So Nagaraj had to while away his time till about seven o'clock when the visitors would be gone and Mother would be back. He loved her company and followed her around as she busied herself in the kitchen and the other parts of the vast house. At the Boardless, Nagaraj always found enjoyable company in his class-fellows, who guffawed and joked till Varma the proprietor sounded a call-bell on his desk to indicate that it was time for them to vacate the table. Coomar, though not a student at any stage in his life, found himself in their company and ordered more coffee for everybody in order to retain the table. When the company dispersed, Coomar stuck to Nagaraj as he walked down Market Road looking at shops and crowds or strolled along the river. Friendship developed between them. Once, years later, Coomar invited Nagaraj into his house at Ellamman Street. It was a narrow little place with a rice store in front, which was their family business. He confided later while they were alone, 'I don't like our family business – selling rice is dull work.'

'What do you plan to do?'

'I don't know – something more active . . .'

'What really do you want to do?' Nagaraj asked sympathetically. Coomar remained silent for some time.

'I do not know. I wish I had gone to school like you. But I was not interested.'

'It doesn't matter,' said Nagaraj grandly, in a sudden access of blind sympathy. 'I myself would not continue but for the compulsion at home. My brother is a model student, very regular in his studies, and so my parents expect me to follow his example . . .'

Coomar felt slightly impatient with the other's rambling

interruption while he was bursting with his own problems and said, 'Parents are all alike. My father wants me to go to school or measure out rice in the shop. I'm prepared to walk out of home if they compel me. I have my own ideas.'

'Tell me,' said Nagaraj, rigorously suppressing his desire to continue his own narration.

'I came across', began Coomar, 'a fellow at the bus stand. He comes from a village nearby, carrying with him a bundle of saris, sells them to the women in the city and goes back to his looms in the village. He is a handloom weaver working at home with his family's help. Cheap cotton saris not costing more than fifteen rupees. At a time three saris are woven on the loom, in a week he can have six saris ready. He comes by bus and spreads them out under a tree and sells them. Whenever I go to the bus stand, I find him there, and I have talked to him – '

'What takes you to the bus stand so regularly?' Nagaraj could not help asking.

Coomar felt irritated again at the interruption but felt obliged to explain: 'Impossible to stay at home, must keep away a greater part of the day, otherwise I'll have to measure out rice . . .' At which both laughed. 'Also I like the Central Bus Stand at South End: full of bustle and activity, with a canteen and waiting hall where one can rest. I know many of the bus folk and often help them in some way. I got an idea one day: why should I not sell those saris rather than our rice? After all, women are ready customers for anything that appeals to them. If I can find two hundred rupees for a start, I can achieve wonders.'

Before the evening was out, Nagaraj fell in with his plans and promised his help. His mother gave him pocket money off and on which he spent at the Boardless for his evening tiffin. His father also gave him money whenever the harvest came. Nagaraj's needs were limited, he never spent the full amount he earned every month. Once a month he took it to the post office on Market Road and put it in the savings bank. He did not recollect the exact amount available but promised Coomar all help.

At their next meeting at the Boardless, when the company was gone, he took Coomar aside and whispered, 'I have two hundred and eighty at the savings bank, I'll give you two hundred, but don't you tell my brother or anyone.' Thus Coomar got a start in business. He kept in touch with the weaver at the bus stand, paid him for six saris at a time with part of the cash. He hired a bicycle from the Rajan Mart every day, tied the bundle of saris on the rack and started off on his sales trip. He had an instinct for the right time and place and the phrase. He never started early his daily rounds: he realised that menfolk should not be present during his visit to a customer in her home. Eleven in the forenoon was an hour most breadwinners in the family would be out. After seeing the man off, the lady of the house would have her meal, chew betel leaves, relax and fall into a shopping mood, especially when the shop was at her door.

On the very first day of the venture, he rode through Kabir Street, leaned his bicycle on the front step and knocked on the door. The door was opened by Nagaraj's mother. Nagaraj, as was his habit even in the early years, was away after his midday meal on a routine visit to Kanni's, and then on to the Town Hall library to be in communion with the librarian. That gave him a feeling of doing research for his magnum opus on Narada, though most of the time was spent sitting on the single stool beside the old librarian's chair exchanging information on the weather, local affairs and the human predicament in general. From time to time he paused to remark, 'There are no authentic references to Narada anywhere and I feel handicapped.'

'Why don't you invent something about the sage?'

'That I can't do. I want to write something which will have authority.'

Nagaraj walked back home and found his friend Coomar squatting in the verandah with all the saris out of the bundle and his wife preoccupied in selecting one. She said, 'Your friend will not leave without selling me a sari.'

'How can I?' said Coomar. 'This is my first business and I know your wife's hand must be lucky . . .'

'Undoubtedly,' said Nagaraj, pleased.

His mother, standing at the door watching the transaction, added, 'These saris seem rather costly and the fabric so thin . . . these days . . .'

The daughter-in-law said, 'Seems to me quite good value. We don't want saris thick as sackcloth.'

'They used to last a lifetime,' Mother retorted.

Nagaraj was anxious to avoid controversy in the presence of his friend. 'Sita, give him something to drink, he has been cycling in the sun.'

Coomar said, 'Just a tumbler of cold water and nothing else. This is my first sale, let me see how lucky your wife's inauguration is going to prove!' Sita fetched from her little shelf in a corner thirty-five rupees for two saris while the old lady kept looking on with disapproval. After Coomar left, Sita whispered to her husband, 'Why should your mother bother? This is my money.'

'You must not take her seriously, she doesn't mean to hurt you.'

When he passed in, his mother began, 'In our days . . .' He didn't encourage her to continue, but said, 'They are going to arrange a forty-day discourse at the temple,' and diverted her talk.

It was an auspicious start for Coomar. He divided the town into convenient sectors and covered the entire city methodically, day by day. He sat down with a sheet of paper in hand, in the little room available to him when his father was away at his shop, and drew a rough map of Malgudi, marking the areas where his customers could be found. He noted: 'East, West, South and North. East: Vinayak Street, Kabir Street. North: New Extension and Lawley Extension, not at present. First cover where they favour cheap saris – maximum price twenty-five rupees. When I get a feeling of the market conditions . . .' Thereafter he started on a cycle with his bundle every day according to schedule.

He knocked on a door, as I have said, when he was sure the men were away. When the door opened and the lady appeared, he said, 'Would you like to see new saris?'

'No,' would be the expected answer, 'I don't want to buy – '

'I never said I'm selling. I just want to show, that's all. Someone suggested that I show you the samples first before they get sold . . .' And as the lady hesitated, he went back to the bicycle and brought out the bundle of saris, laid it at her feet and spread out his wares. When he left he would have sold at least one sari. On the rare occasion when a man happened to open the door and say point-blank, 'No one is buying any sari . . .'

'But amma has asked me to come – new patterns.' At this point the lady of the house would come on the scene. Before the man could question, 'Did you ask to see a sari?' Coomar had spread and displayed his wares, saying, 'No harm in having a look at these. No need to buy . . .'

'What is the price?' would be the next question.

'If you like the stuff, make your choice, do not bother about the price . . .' By the time he had bundled up and started on his rounds again, he would have made one more sale and collected the cash.

At the end of the day he went to the bus stand, met the weaver and ordered the next lot – at this stage only the twenty-five rupee variety. He felt encouraged to offer clients costlier saris in course of time. He contacted a silk weaver in another village and acquired saris of one-hundred-rupee value. He ordered only four at a time; cycling was easier with only four in a bundle. He tried other zones – Lawley Extension, New Extension, and a new housing colony beyond the railway crossing. At the end of the day he met Nagaraj at the Boardless for help in writing up the accounts.

He stopped going in search of custom. Coomar's name became well known when he took a small shop on Market Road. Eventually he returned the two-hundred-rupee loan to Nagaraj, bought the house at the corner of Grove Street and opened the big shop.

Nagaraj felt gratified that the small loan he managed to give had taken Coomar such a long way. When Raman, the painter, had finally fixed the sign board on the arch at the gate, they stood away in the middle of Grove Street and surveyed it with satisfaction. Raman had imparted colour and design to COOMAR'S BOEING SARI CENTRE. Coomar took Raman in and seated him on the carpet and offered him five hundred rupees tucked amidst green betel leaves, two coconuts and a bunch of bananas on a tray. Raman accepted it gratefully and took his leave. Nagaraj said, 'Good style . . . I mean your payment.'

'Goddess Lakshmi has been kind,' was all that Coomar was to say.

Now Nagaraj uttered the question that had been bothering him all along. 'Why Boeing? What is it?'

Coomar himself was not clear in his mind about it. So he said, 'It's a name which I noticed on a paper wrapped round a yarn sample, and it appealed to me somehow.'

After Kanni's, the retreat to the Grove Street Sari Centre was very pleasant. A spreading margosa tree afforded a cool shade to the building, and Nagaraj found it agreeable and interesting to work for Coomar. The Boeing Centre had become one of the established institutions of Malgudi. All day it was crowded with shoppers, mainly women, who spent hours and hours choosing saris. Weavers from the loom areas thronged to gain Coomar's patronage. It was always reputed that Coomar's saris were created especially for Malgudi women: the stamp of Coomar meant fast colours and unfading lace of the finest gold-coated silver.

'I want you to look over my business and give me your

suggestions,' Coomar said one day, and set up a table and chair for Nagaraj at one end of the hall while he himself sat cross-legged on a cushion on the floor, leaning on a bolster. The Sari Centre was a big hall stacked with saris in almirahs all round. Carpets and mats covered the floor, wall to wall, and several assistants pulled out saris from the racks and spread them out on the mats for inspection by customers who, unlike customers of other kinds of business, settled down for the day and relaxed.

Attendants heaped on his table registers and ledgers and cash bills, which Nagaraj scrutinised and entered in the appropriate column in his books. He loved this work, alternating red ink and black ink while entering figures. He picked up special penholders at Bari's – paper merchants and stationers at Kalighat Lane which cut across Market Road at some point westward. He loved the stationery shop with its smell of gum and paper and display of pens and pencils under a glass.

'I import pens the like of which you can't see anywhere,' the stationer would claim, being in business second generation on the same spot. 'You might have heard of Hamilton Bond. It's world famous – the best in the world. The chief of that concern was Sir Richard Hamilton, whose signed portrait adorns the wall of our home, which is nearby. He gave it to my grandfather and even today the firm sends us goods on credit without any condition. Is that possible now with others? Impossible, sir. We settle the bills promptly on the sixtieth day . . .' He seemed to Nagaraj like a non-stop gramophone with the needle coming back to the starting point every time to begin all over again.

'This chap's musical refrain is Hamilton. He will not let me examine penholders in peace . . .' Nagaraj loved coloured penholders – green, red, yellow and brown, with nibs in different styles. He would prefer to be left alone to make his choice. The Boeing Sari Centre was a place of colour, a riot of blue and red and mauve and green as saris were spread out on the mats, and he did not like to hold a pen which might be incongruous in this seeming flower bed of a million hues. But the lean paper-fellow would not leave him in peace, dressed as he always was in a white jibba and jodhpur trousers and an embroidered cap, dogging his steps and chattering about Hamilton.

Coomar had asked him to choose the best stationery he liked and he explained, 'Our Boeing Centre is unique and has distinction, and our stationery must not be inferior. Go ahead and choose without fear or hesitation about the prices.'

'A liberal allowance,' Nagaraj thought. 'But why are these merchants so conceited and talkative, each man thinking he is a special brand of God's creation?'

Nagaraj worked free for Coomar; no pay packet at the beginning of a month. 'I don't need it, and this arrangement leaves me free to come and go when I like, though this bandicoot can afford to pay me, considering that he collects two thousand rupees an hour from those sari-crazed chatter-boxes, and I don't know what he does with all that cash.'

Facilitated thus by a lack of arrangement, Nagaraj appeared at the Centre regularly but without a feeling of compulsion, and left when he liked, and Coomar never said a word, being politic and enjoying Nagaraj's free services.

Nagaraj liked to be out of the house as far as possible, otherwise he might have to arbitrate between his mother and Sita all day. He sometimes wondered at the transformations time brings about.

Sita was a timid little creature when he married her. How many years ago? He threw his mind back almost twenty years. When he went to approve his bride at their house in Sullivan Street, she looked so small and helpless. At first he felt discouraged. He was under twenty and she was fourteen and looked as if she had just come out of the nursery school. Her personality had not yet developed. Her obscure features could not give one an idea whether she was good looking or not. She had a rotund face, a scraggy slight figure and a long, long braid, with a wheaten complexion over which some kind of face powder stood out challengingly. During that bride-inspection she had to demonstrate her musical ability with a harmonium and sang some song in a feeble voice. Nagaraj, though he could not make up his mind, was favourably inclined. He had just passed his B.A. exam and was himself stocky and dark complexioned and never hoped he could command a glamorous bride. His qualification was not his personality but his family – that was his Kabir Street home and background, people who were considered aristocratic inheritors of vast rice fields in the village. Sita's father was a retired government servant and was recommended by a well-wisher of both the families. Nagaraj's father could not hope for a better connection, since he was convinced that Nagaraj was wishy-washy and dreamy – a view that he held to the last.

In the early days Nagaraj found his wife too timid and bashful. His mother in those days was like a commander-in-chief and the girl meekly accepted the role of a lackey at home, forever at the beck and call of her mother-in-law, trailing behind her all the time, hardly ever coming into his room while he longed for a tête-à-tête. When she came in she never allowed the door to be shut fully but always left a crack open. 'Mother may not like it,' 'Mother may want to call me,' 'She is all alone in the kitchen, I must be near at hand, she may mistake me . . .'

'Mistake? What sort of mistake – after all, you will be talking to your husband . . .' She hardly gave him her company with a free heart. And he took to the pyol habit, to sitting there and watching the street. In the evenings when Mother went to the temple at the corner, Sita relaxed and came to him. She would not sit down for fear that the neighbours might gossip. Nagaraj would try to hold her hand or pull her down to his side. She resisted and drew herself away out of his reach, whereupon he would protest, 'After all you are my wife, what is wrong?'

'Don't talk so loudly – hush, this is not our room.' She would stand beside him fidgeting, allowing enough space between to make onlookers think that the couple were semi-strangers. Nagaraj accepted the arrangement as inevitable. He could not make any demand on her or anyone. Not in his nature. At a discreet distance from each other, they would discuss the day's events from the time she was up at six a.m. till the moment Mother went down to the temple. How she put the kettle on for coffee, how she almost toppled down the filter while pouring into it boiling water. How lucky Mother was not there! 'She had gone out to fetch wood chips from the back yard. When she came in she could see nothing more than some water spilled on the floor and asked for an explanation. I explained it away somehow, and Mother did not bother about it any more . . .' Nagaraj simpered as if he admired Sita's pluck and resourcefulness, although he did not quite understand what she had done. He added irrelevantly, 'Be careful while handling the boiling water.' They watched for a while in silence the neighbours' children playing in the street and the women returning home from their shopping and visits, throwing sidelong glances at the couple on the pyol. 'People are returning from the temple, Mother'll be here soon . . .' said Sita, turning to go in.

Nagaraj would implore, 'Stay,' and try to hold her.

'She told me to grate half a coconut for chutney. She will be upset,' said Sita. Suddenly she would wrench herself free and run in so that when Mother returned she would see him alone and, even while climbing the steps, ask, 'Where is Sita?'

'I think she is scraping coconut, judging from the noise inside . . .' he would say with an innocent look. Mother would hold out a little vermilion and sacred ash – offerings from the temple – and then go in, pleased at the dutifulness of her daughter-in-law.

After his graduation, Gopu spurned Nagaraj and ordered him about. Nagaraj did not mind it. He continued to be a devoted younger brother.

'You are like Lakshmana in the Ramayana, who stood behind Rama, his elder brother, all the time without a murmur or doubt,' remarked his father sometimes. It was no doubt flattering, but it didn't help the younger man very much. The brothers shared the front room in the Kabir Street house; the room in the other wing was occupied by Father and Mother. His mother slept on the floor, while Father occupied the teakwood four-poster which filled the space in the room. When the sons came up to the college level, Mother preferred to go out and sleep in the second courtyard in summer. In the cooler season she slept in the hall. When Gopu's fame as a graduate spread, letters of marriage offers came enclosing horoscopes from parents who had daughters. And Father spent much time in scrutinising and comparing the charts and finally approved one, the daughter of a 'sub-registrar' from Sembiam, said to be wealthy and influential in that area (the sub-registrar, unofficially, levied a percentage as his share on any property registered and collected much cash from unlettered villagers who were at his mercy).

They locked up the Kabir Street house and chartered a whole bus for the wedding trip. It was a grand occasion, a six-hour journey northward after crossing the river at Nallapa's grove. Nagaraj often recollected with pleasure the occasion as they carried eatables and spiced rice and curds, fruits in large quantity, enough to feed the party of forty relatives and friends in the bus. Nagaraj enjoyed the endless eating all the way. It was very pleasant on the whole. His brother also seemed to thaw a bit. The prospect of his wedding softened him and he chatted with Nagaraj all through the journey and joked and laughed. To Nagaraj, who was already in a state of elation, his brother's patronage was an added pleasure. He kept on humbly agreeing with all that he said, and laughed at his lugubrious jokes as the bus sped along the countryside through coconut avenues and cattle herds, and for some time the babble and chatter among the company resounded over the noise of the running bus. It was a long journey – enough time for them to talk, eat and fall asleep in their seats or lapse into silence, watching the scenery.

When Gopu's wife joined him at Kabir Street about a year later, Nagaraj had to vacate his corner in the front room. Gopu just said, 'Boy, leave my room.' Nagaraj picked up his books and pushed out his dealwood box in which he had kept an assortment of possessions – tinsel pieces, picture books and pencils and clothes. He moved his desk to a corner in the hall. Now his brother isolated himself and kept to his room all day, but his wife emerged periodically and went in again, shutting the door, leaving Nagaraj to speculate what might be going on inside. Gopu did not seem keen on working anywhere after acquiring his B.A. His father hinted from time to time, 'Now that you are a B.A., it will be easy to get a job. Shall I speak to Mr Menon, our District Collector, who knows a lot of people and will help?'

'Not necessary,' was Gopu's only answer. He showed no inclination to go out of the house or seek work. Father let things drift, unable to divine the other's intention, while he shut himself away with his wife.

All the time Nagaraj sat in the allotted corner of the hall

trying to concentrate on his studies, sitting on the floor. They had only two folding chairs in the house, one in his brother's room and one in his father's. Nagaraj had been offered another room in the second courtyard but he preferred to stay in the hall in order that he might watch the traffic there. Watching and speculating what went on behind the door was more interesting than homework. While appearing to be reading his lessons he noted from a corner of his eye his sister-in-law bearing a dish of some eatable to their room, perhaps almond fried in butter with a sprinkling of sugar. After his marriage his brother fancied himself a sultan in his palace chamber, pampered by his wife. Nagaraj also noted how long it took for his brother to eat the stuff. He saw by the old ticking clock on the opposite wall that Gopu consumed whatever came in about twelve minutes. His mouth watered at the thought and he wondered what it could be, bonda or halwa. Was it sweet or sour? He could not hope to have a taste of it since it was a special preparation created at a special stove which had been commissioned for the sultan in a specially reserved corner of the general kitchen where his mother had cooked for the entire family from the beginning of time (as it seemed). The sultan's spouse concocted specialities for her husband in strictly limited quantities, of which others could enjoy only the fragrance emanating from the stove.

'Why couldn't I have it too?' Nagaraj asked his mother. 'What is it that sister-in-law makes for Gopu?'

'None of your business to talk about it.'

'But I want it too.'

'She goes herself to Chettiar's shop, buys something and comes home. Never heard of any young woman going out to a shop by herself. She has brought from her parents' house her own stove and vessels, and gives her husband what she likes. I never look at her corner of the kitchen.'

'Why don't you make the same thing for us too?'

'All right, all right,' she said to mollify him. 'Now you eat this . . .' When she got a feeling that Gopu was dependent solely on his wife, she would offer her creation to the daughter-in-law. 'Let Gopu taste this too. He will like it . . .' Sometimes the daughter-in-law would agree and carry a dish to his room, but more often say, 'No, Mother, don't trouble yourself. He'll not eat it.' It was a state within the state.

Nagaraj noticed that the two managed their jurisdictions with tact. Sister-in-law Charu was allotted her corner of the kitchen along the eastern wall. She set up a little stool, and mounted a kerosene stove on it and beside it a little platform on which she arranged a set of aluminium saucepans and ladles, etc., and she stood over her workshop, frying and sizzling delicacies for her husband. This position had the advantage that she could work with her back to her mother-in-law, who squatted on the floor in front of her mud oven at the other end, which was an age-old equipment of her kitchen. It was built once a year with the clay dug from the back yard, kneaded and moulded into an oven.

Mother believed that food cooked over smoky firewood in the mud oven was healthful while a kerosene flame caused throat trouble. To prove it she blew her nose and sneezed when Charu lit her kerosene stove. Charu ignored these symptoms and said, 'Mother, a wood fire leads to cold and eye disease, that's what my mother used to say . . .' and she managed without going in for wood fuel but used only kerosene or charcoal, thus tactfully puncturing her mother-in-law's notions about the kerosene stove. If mother-in-law asked, 'What are you preparing?' Charu only mumbled without turning round, and if the mother-in-law repeated her question, she mumbled again persistently. After the first few days she ignored all queries and communicated only when it pleased her. 'This time of the year, carrots are in plenty,' Charu might deign to remark occasionally, facing her wall. At which the mother-in-law would feel so pleased that she would elaborate on the state of vegetables and try to stretch the conversation out. 'Well, go and tell Gopu that plates are laid and we are waiting.'

If her mood was right, Charu would fetch her husband from the room to join the family at the meal. His sitting plank would be placed beside the door and there he always sat, after throwing a word of greeting to his mother, which was enough to thrill her, seeing so little of him all day. His father sat as always at his allotted seat below the first window. Mother served them. Nagaraj had his position of vantage below the second window. Being the junior-most, he was served last, but being Mother's pet, she served vegetables and rice liberally until he protested and Father came to his rescue saying, 'Just give him what he wants, he is old enough, don't overload his plate.' His brother ate in silence, he was not particularly friendly with his father, as he suspected that if he relented Father would renew his offer to take him to the influential collector to find him a job, and it seemed to the observant Nag that he nipped Father's proposal in the bud while Charu kept a watch on his plate and served with measured caution. She took from her mother-in-law's preparations just a small quantity of some item of food and served her husband for the sake of appearances so that it might not seem as if she ignored completely the food meant for the family. The family ate in general silence, only Nagaraj trying to keep up a conversation, undeterred by the absence of response from the rest of the family. He laughed and cracked jokes and narrated his school incidents, unmindful of the indifference of others. Only his mother pretended to listen and appreciate what he said, but always concluded, 'Eat, eat, don't keep talking . . .'

At this stage, when fragments of memory brought back pictures of other people and other days, all that load of experience seemed improbable to Nagaraj. His mother now hobbled about like a frail ghost asking inane questions of the two left at home, himself and his wife; only three in that vast household which stretched from Kabir Street to the river. Mother perambulated about the house unnecessarily, as it seemed to Nagaraj, with weak legs and minimal energy, and she would not rest, although provided with a fan and a cot in the hall.

The old lady kept inspecting and watching every corner of the house and commenting, to the annoyance of Nagaraj's wife who often burst out, 'Please keep your mother in one place. I feel paralysed when she is following me about, questioning and questioning – I can't cook or sweep or clean if I'm bothered like this.' Nagaraj had more tolerance than his wife.

'After all, she is asking some questions, give some answer and be done with it – '

'How many times can I face the same set of questions?'

'As often as necessary,' Nagaraj said and fled from the scene before his wife could retort.

Mother's decline started with Father's death. The fifteenth day after his father's funeral the mourning period was over and all the purificatory ceremonials were gone through. It was past two in the afternoon when the last guest departed after an elaborate feast and the family members were left to themselves. Nagaraj was getting ready to shut himself in his room and sleep. His wife was putting back the vessels on the shelf and sweeping the floor clean of flowers and shreds of banana leaves and spilled food, sharing silently the labours of winding up. The cooks engaged for the feast were taking leave of Nagaraj's mother, who was lost in her own thoughts, leaning on a pillar in the courtyard, away from all company. She was clad in a simple white sari, without lace, and with all jewellery removed, although when her husband was living she used to be radiant with diamonds and clad in gold-laced saris, never going below a certain standard of dress and decoration, so that the neighbours always remarked, 'She's like Goddess Lakshmi and rules the family like a queen!' Some called her vain and showy – 'Wants to impress us with her diamonds and brocade. We know how this family came to be rich – moneylenders, actually . . .'

Nagaraj felt deeply moved by her withdrawal and from

time to time went near her to whisper a word of comfort or philosophy. Nagaraj was saying, 'Mother, why don't you go in and rest? Visitors are gone – I'll also turn in for a couple of hours' rest in my room – ' Gopu overheard Nag's words and said at once, 'Nagu, don't try to go away. I've business with you. Come to my room.'

Thus it started. For a month to come, every hour of the day was occupied in drawing up a list of assets, properties, possessions and articles left by his father. He had left a will, which simply declared, 'Everything I have to be divided equally between my two sons unless they come to some agreement suitable to their needs.' A lawyer friend of the family was to help them come to a decision. Gopu stuck to the expression in the will, 'Some arrangement suitable, etc. . . .', declaring, 'Father himself was aware that equal division was unsuitable – I can't accept anything unless there is a fresh valuation.' Thereafter every item was listed and valued. Such things were beyond Nagaraj's temperament and capacity. They inspected room by room, and every item in the household went into the list 'except the broomstick', as his mother declared when she recovered her mood and speech. Nagaraj's own inclination was to accept whatever came in as his share, but his brother was aggressive and demanding. He insisted upon being given all the land and coconut garden in the village along with the farmhouse and cattle. 'Thank God the fellow wants them. I couldn't have stood the smell of cattleshed even for five minutes . . .' thought Nagaraj.

'What have you to say?' asked the lawyer.

Nagaraj did not want to say anything, having no ideas of his own, and maintained a pregnant silence which the lawyer took to be a state of profound thinking on his part.

His brother lost his patience and cried, 'Nag, understand there is no other way.'

Nagaraj looked despondent and bit his lips and shot off at a tangent. 'What happens to Mother's jewellery?'

'The question does not arise now,' said the lawyer pompously. 'Only to be decided at the appropriate time.'

'What do you mean?' asked Nagaraj, looking outraged and feeling that he should not let the others have their own way. He suspected the lawyer was being bribed by his brother, although he had been his father's chum. His strategy produced results. In return for surrendering his interests in the village holding, he was to have the Kabir Street house as the sole owner. Nagaraj asked, 'What about Mother?'

'Let her have her choice,' pronounced the lawyer. 'After all, only two sons – she'd like to be with one or the other and move when she needs a change.'

'Very well put,' said Gopu.

'All this presupposes that the brothers live separately,' added the lawyer. 'Am I right?'

Gopu went red in the face as he asserted, 'I won't stay here a day after the documents are signed. Who wants to be here? Not my family.'

It only confirmed Nagaraj's suspicion that Gopu's wife was the prompter behind the scene, planning to get away from the mother-in-law.

At the end of the month the partition deed was drawn and signed and registered. Packing up all his share of silver, brass utensils, miscellaneous articles and furniture, and odds and ends (with the exception of the oval silver plate and the wall mirror which Nagaraj stubbornly would not yield), Gopu never knew Nag could be so firm in any matter. After consulting a priest, a day was fixed and a van stood at the door. Gopu loaded all his share, prostrated at Mother's feet and left with his family, while his mother looked on sadly and asked constantly, 'Was this all necessary?' She shed tears at the parting. Nagaraj himself felt overwhelmed. He ran a few yards clutching the door when the van moved, crying to his brother, 'Leave Tim behind, not too late even now. St Stephen's is a good school. I'll look after him – '

His brother just said, 'No, he will be with me.'

Nagaraj was heartbroken.

On the few occasions when Nagaraj visited his brother at the village, he noticed Tim going to a 'pyol school' – that was a sort of mud platform canopied with thatch and straw and presided over by the local pedagogue who conducted his classes by shouting and flourishing his cane at the children who squatted before him. This teaching method was much appreciated by the village elders, who based their educational philosophy on the proverb, 'The unbeaten child will remain unlearned.' Nagaraj felt sickened: a far cry from St Stephen's in Malgudi, which was a coveted school where Tim was admitted by Nagaraj when the brothers lived together in Kabir Street as an undivided family; and definitely worse than the derelict municipal school in which he and his brother had studied as children. He did not talk about it for fear of irritating Gopu. Luckily the shed collapsed during a storm, and the platform was washed off; the pedagogue could not rebuild it.

Thus ended the educational career of the village children, who turned to performing odd tasks on their farms. Gopu, however, sent Tim to a town school five miles away. The boy had to walk a mile to catch a highway bus after waiting for it under an avenue tree. It was tedious. Some days, if the bus arrived late, he missed it deliberately, since he did not like to be caned for going late to his class. So he just dawdled and wandered about and marked time till he could go back home. Some days, if a bus going in the direction of Malgudi came up, he jumped into it and secretly visited his uncle at Kabir Street. He enjoyed his visits to his uncle as he was received with warmth and fêted in their house. Nagaraj saved the boy embarrassment by not questioning him too closely about his movements but took care to return him to his village in the evening bus.

It was a busy hour at the Sari Centre, which meant the noisiest moment with customers, all women, discussing the worth of various types and patterns and their suitability for occasions. Nagaraj was quite used to this din. He could go on with his accounting and entries without feeling disturbed. He sat in his corner bent over his papers, and did not hear the call from across his table, 'Uncle! I've come – ' When he looked up he saw Tim standing before him. He almost rubbed his eyes to be sure that it was no apparition.

'Tim! Why did you not tell me you were coming?' Nagaraj put away his books, wiped the pen with the rag which was always in its place on his desk under a glass paperweight. He locked up the ledgers, murmured to Tim again, 'Sit down on that stool. I'll be with you in a minute.'

Nagaraj sensed that this was unlike other visits by Tim. The boy, who usually looked bright and happy during his visits, now looked glum and only muttered, when questioned, 'I've come away with my trunk.' What was the significance of the mention of trunk? Nagaraj suspected some complication back at the village and only said, 'Wait, sit on that stool. I'll be with you soon.' In a little while he went to Coomar, said something, and joined his nephew.

'Let's go,' he said. The boy stood up and gazed with wonder at the crowd of women and the colourful saris spread on the mat. Carrying his small trunk, Tim accompanied Nagaraj home. They walked silently. Nagaraj was afraid to open his mouth lest some impossible situation should reveal itself.

Sita, opening the door, was surprised to see Tim. Nagaraj said inanely, 'He is come with his trunk.' While he went in to change and wash, she took charge of Tim and his trunk, and gave him coffee and tiffin, and decided not to question him. Nagaraj's mother was in a far corner of the house in the second courtyard, on her routine wandering, and was not yet aware of her grandson's arrival.

When Nagaraj was ready for a talk, he felt a little anxious and nervous. He seated Tim on the pyol and asked, 'Now, tell me what happened. Why are you carrying your trunk?'

'Because I am not going back – '

'Oh!' exclaimed Nagaraj, rather pleased. 'Surely . . . But does your father know?'

'He should know, he saw me walking out with the trunk.'

Nagaraj realised that the boy attached some extraordinary significance to the trunk. He remained silent; some neighbours passing down the street noticed them conversing and slowed down their pace, hoping to overhear their talk. The executive engineer of the last house, returning from the bar, cried on seeing Tim, 'Hallo! How you have grown, like the eucalyptus tree which stood around my office in the hills. Say namasthe to your elders,' and passed on.

Tim volunteered to explain, 'He called me a donkey – '

'Who?'

'Father.'

'Why?' Nagaraj asked aloud, but added within, 'Why not?'

The boy explained, 'He asked me to go to the fields and report to him on the work people were doing. I hesitated, I had to go out to catch the bus otherwise I would be punished for going late. He called me "donkey". I said, "What's a donkey, Father?" and he slapped my face. My mother was away.'

'Otherwise what would have happened?' Nagaraj asked, his curiosity stirred as to how Charu would confront her husband. He asked, 'Does your mother . . . ?' He could not find the right word. He swallowed back the phrase, 'Quarrel with him?' It would have been very pleasing to hear that she did, but he changed his sentence to 'Did she tell you what to do?'

The boy was rather puzzled at the nature of the enquiry, and said, 'I packed up my trunk and left. Mother was returning just as I was leaving. I met her on the way and told her, "I'm going to Malgudi and will not be back." She asked many questions but I could not answer them. She tried to hold me back and snatched away my trunk but I shook myself free and ran, crying, "I won't come back. Don't wait . . ." '

Nagaraj felt confused by this muddled account and said, 'Stay here by all means. I'll be happy . . .' He felt his brother was likely to turn up sooner or later and worsen the situation. He felt a terrible responsibility had fallen on him.

Nagaraj was sitting on the pyol, spending the evening as usual looking at the coconut trees with crows retiring for the night. Before repairing to the trees they assembled on the roof of the tall house in the opposite row. Scores of them flew down and perched like schoolchildren under the supervision of a convent sister. The crows argued a lot among themselves and hopped and shifted about before dispersing. Nagaraj always felt a fascination for this evening activity of the crows, and wished he knew the language of birds as did the kings of folklore. The crows probably have a leader who allots them treetops for the night and they argue and debate about it before coming to a decision. The leader would probably be saying, 'Don't you see the sky is reddening? Hurry up, darkness will soon be upon us, and remember we are not human beings who light lamps for their night life . . .'

This fantasy was shattered when a jutka halted in front of him, wheels crunching the gravel. He could not believe his eyes: his brother emerged from the jutka. As he stepped down, all the pent-up affection in Nagaraj burst forth, 'Oh, Gopu, come, come. Why didn't you write to me you were coming? I'd have met you at the bus stand – you came by bus?'

'How else? Did you expect me to come in an aeroplane from our village?'

'Why not? Within ten years you may have plane service all over . . .'

'Don't talk nonsense!' Gopu said. He picked up his bag and, thrusting his hand into the inner pocket of a tight buttoned-up grey coat (which Nagaraj had known him possess for years), fished out an eight-anna coin to pay the fare. The jutka driver did not close his fingers on the coin but kept staring at Gopu accusingly. 'That's all. Go,' thundered Gopu. 'The avarice of these fellows has no limit.'

'Grass sells at ten annas a bundle. How can I feed the horse and myself?'

'Go away, I don't care,' cried Gopu. 'These fellows in Malgudi are spoilt by outsiders. Go, you won't get a paisa more,' whereupon Nagaraj took out of a fold at his waist in his dhoti four annas and counted it out on the man's outstretched palm. Glaring at the brothers without speaking, the driver declared the general meanness of Kabir Street dwellers, whipped his horse and moved off. Gopu said, 'You are spoiling these fellows. Why did you pay, as if I couldn't afford it? I want to teach these blackguards in Malgudi a lesson.'

'Life is too short for teaching lessons – '

'You and your philosophy,' sneered Gopu, and asked, 'Where is Tim?'

'Gone out,' said Nagaraj, somewhat nervously.

'It's six-thirty! And he is not home yet!' cried Gopu acidly.

'Come in first, have a wash and eat something, and then I will tell you. Come in first. Plenty of time. What time did you leave?'

Gopu ignored the question and said, 'I'm going back in the morning and he must come with me.'

'Where is the hurry?' Nagaraj asked apprehensively.

'He is my son and has to be with me, that's all. I'm not bound to explain. I've tolerated his ways too long,' he said, raising his voice.

'I'm thinking of admitting him at Albert Mission . . .'

'What for? Did you have the sense to ask me first?'

Nagaraj had no reply to this, a part of his mind admiring his wife's cautioning him. She had said, when Nagaraj spoke of it, 'Don't rush without consulting your brother about Tim's studies. He may not like you to take upon yourself all that.'

And Nagaraj had tried to silence her with, 'You always think negatively. I know what to do with Tim.'

And she went away with a toss of her head, saying, 'Surely you know your brother – after all, aren't you brothers?'

'She has uncanny forethought,' he said to himself now. 'I should hereafter leave everything to her – all management and decisions.'

'What are you muttering to yourself, while you have nothing to say to me, and stand there blinking and mumbling like a schoolboy,' sneered Gopu.

Nagaraj realised he could not very well confess that he was secretly admiring Sita's wisdom. 'Come in. Sita will be back from the temple soon. Evenings she visits the temple.'

'Are you trying to divert my thoughts? Tell me first, where is Tim?'

They were both standing on the doorstep. The ex-engineer living in the last house was tottering back from the bar at the market. He halted in front of the house and said, 'Where is my wife? I'm wifeless but not yet a widower, sir. Pity me and yield her if you have kept her here.'

Gopu said, 'Oh, this fellow still going strong! Let's go in.' He turned and went in. Nagaraj led the way, and first took him to Tim's room, flinging the door open. 'You remember we used to be here. Now Tim is in this room.'

'Where is Mother? How is she?' asked Gopu. Nagaraj led him to his mother's room in the second courtyard. He whispered, 'These days she retires before sunset and wakes up before midnight and keeps calling everybody, thinking it is morning.' Gopu stood on the threshold of her darkened room and, finding her asleep, withdrew, saying, 'I will see her later before I leave.'

Sita had meanwhile returned from the temple quietly, without a sound, as a courtesy to her husband's elder brother. Gopu sat in his chair while Nagaraj kept standing. She stood in the doorway and asked, 'Shall I make coffee? Give me five minutes. I was delayed as there was a Friday crowd with their offerings.'

'I had coffee on the way at the canteen in the bus stand.'

'If I'd known you were coming – a postcard would have been enough . . .' She was acting the part of junior sister-in-law (younger brother's wife) perfectly. Gopu appreciated it. Whatever might be his attitude to his brother, he was always gentle with Sita. After the formal welcome she withdrew to prepare a dinner befitting the visitor. Before going she somehow managed to signal to her husband and he quietly got up and followed her. In the hall she whispered, 'What shall I make? Should you not have warned me? How can I manage if you sit back as if you were a guest?'

'Be quick and do something,' he said. 'I know you can . . .' He turned round and re-entered the room.

Meanwhile Gopu had taken off his shirt and coat and uppercloth and heaped them on the chair. He settled himself comfortably and remarked, 'So late, and Tim hasn't come yet! You let him loaf like this!'

'He goes out and comes home,' Nagaraj explained.

'Where does he go? Don't you have to keep an eye?'

Nagaraj realised his inability to do such a thing and grinned awkwardly. Gopu glared at him in anger, 'You are strange, impossible. You have no idea what to do, where and when. You exist from day to day like a cow chewing the cud and staring at space . . .'

Nagaraj felt uncomfortable and laughed nervously, treating it as a joke.

Gopu said, 'Whatever may be the reason, he will have to

come back with me, that's all. You should have turned him round and sent him to the village on the first day. Instead of that . . .'

Nagaraj had a sinking feeling at the prospect of Tim going away and said, 'I'll see that he comes to the village later.'

'Do you think I'm here to ask for a favour? I can handle him myself. Except these few days, I was the one to handle him. What do you know of boys? If he is growing in your shadow, he will be another Nagaraj. We do not want another Nagaraj in the family.' And he laughed bitterly. Nagaraj was unaffected by this attack, took it all as an expression of Gopu's sense of humour and goodwill. He got up abruptly to go out of the room under the pretext of finding if dinner was ready. His brother, now settled on the easy chair in the room, said, 'Don't get up and try to escape. You have not lost that habit yet! Listen to me. You should have turned him back on the very first day. Instead of that you petted and pampered him, without even asking whether he took my permission before leaving home.'

'Yes, I asked him whether he had your – '

'What did he say?'

'I don't remember,' Nagaraj said.

'I want him with me. I'm adding so many things to our farm – I don't have to explain to you, but anyway you must understand the situation. Also his mother misses him and is crying all the time. He must share my labours and assist me, a grown-up boy must make himself useful. I'm putting up a gas plant which can function with the cattle refuse, which is in plenty with forty animals in the shed – the gas plant will give us light and fuel. My wife has eye trouble now, cooking with firewood, kerosene being scarce, and the smoke has affected her eyes. Also we could have gas lights.'

'Very interesting, but why disturb Tim? He is happy here.'

'If you have not realised why, I don't have to tell you

anything more. Even this I have said too much for a fellow like you.'

At this point they had to go and eat. Gopu ate in silence, not wishing to exhibit his irritation before Sita. Sita had managed to provide betel leaves and arecanut on a silver plate for chewing after dinner. Gopu and Nagaraj sat on the bench in the hall and were chewing with the contentment that comes with good food followed by proper betel-chewing.

At ten o'clock Tim knocked on the door. Gopu rushed up to open it, gazed on Tim, and said, 'After all, you found your way home!'

Tim was called in by Sita to eat.

'Is this the hour daily when he comes?' asked Gopu, and added in an undertone, 'You should spank him.'

'No, no,' Nagaraj said, shocked, and added rather idiotically, 'See how tall he has grown!' while his mind clamoured to clear the point as to what made him call Tim 'donkey'.

Tim remained silent while his father was telling him to pack up. Nagaraj felt unequal to the situation. He was afraid that Gopu might assault his son or call him 'donkey' again. If he repeated that awful explosive term, God knew what would happen. He feared that the boy might hit back in some terrible manner. He wished he could don his ochre robe and retreat into the puja room, dead for the hour, away from all strife. 'Why don't you get ready? We leave early in the morning,' shouted Gopu.

All that the boy said was, 'No, I'm staying here. I may come there for a few days, later, but now I want to be here. I am not coming home.'

Gopu let out a sigh of despair, unable to do anything else. Nagaraj felt happy to see Gopu, who always had the last word, now helpless. His aggressiveness, conceit and sharp tongue were gone. Nagaraj felt like crying out to Tim, 'Well done, my boy!' but remained silent, looking appropriately solemn. Gopu tried to change his tone. Tried persuasion. Mentioned his mother and her crying. It was also hard for Nagaraj to imagine Charu crying, she who had been so imperious and self-assured as the senior daughter-in-law of the family years ago. Nothing moved Tim. He was adamant. He just kept saying, 'I'll come later and see Mother. I want to be here.'

Next morning Gopu left in a rage, without saying goodbye, carrying his bag and walking off to find a jutka at the market corner, Nagaraj following him meekly. Gopu said, 'You go back. You have spoilt him beyond repair: you are Narada, mischief-maker. If he doesn't want to see me, I don't want to see his face either,' and went down the street briskly as Nagaraj turned back home.

Nagaraj was happy that Gopu had called him Narada abusively. He took it as a compliment. 'Narada created strife, no doubt, by passing disturbing gossip from one quarter to another, but it always proved beneficial in the long run, in an eternal perspective. Must write about him from this angle. Must write in English, of course, so that the book is widely read and people understand the concept of Narada. Must start writing on a good day like Vijayadasami, the day of the Goddess of Learning. But I'm not a writer, must be helped by someone in the line. Must consult the Talkative Man, if I can stop him for a moment when he emerges from his home while starting on his rounds. Or Professor Lingham of Albert Mission School.'

Returning, he didn't enter the house but sat on the pyol to contemplate further on Narada. 'The problem was that there was no authoritative source. Narada's birth was controversial. He would take him as one that just happened to be, that was all and that was sufficient. All that mattered was that he was a unique personality, the god of music. He was ever-cheerful and active, always with a song on his lips, and moved with ease among gods and demons. Blessed with extreme mobility, he traversed at a thought the skies and space, through galaxies and the Milky Way, and was welcome in all the fourteen worlds above and below this world. Gods and demons alike were friendly to him, although he was a bearer of gossip from one world to another and created strife. Wait till I write my book.' He addressed his brother mentally, sending his thoughts to the bus stand.

CHAPTER 4

Going back to the past, Sita's association with Tim had begun on that day her sister-in-law brought him from her parents' home as a three-month-old baby. She took charge of him and showered on him all the maternal love bottled up within her, being childless. She bathed the child, changed his clothes and nursed him, leaving Charu free to attend to her husband's needs, embroider or read magazines by the light in the back courtyard. Her mother-in-law never ordered her or commented on her activities, as she felt slightly awed in her presence and also grateful to her for bearing a child, unlike Sita.

Various measures to cure barrenness had been suggested to Sita by her mother-in-law, who fancied herself an expert, having inherited medical knowledge from her herbalist grandfather. She would sit before Sita in the verandah of the third courtyard to supervise her chewing of neem leaves every morning, and at that time would also regale her with reminiscences.

'I remember how double-bullock carts arrived to fetch my grandfather to distant corners of the country. He must have cured thousands of cases of barrenness, and I used to enjoy the day-long rides with Grandfather. I can still hear the jingling of the bells around the necks of trotting bullocks. He would not ride in anything less than a double-bullock carriage with proper cushions. If anyone sent an ordinary bullock-cart with a straw-covered seat, he would not come out of his room but ask me or my sister to send away the caller. And many women remained barren thereafter, for he was a determined soul. Once he said, "No," it remained "No," even if the heavens pleased.'

At some stage, Sita refused to eat any more neem leaves, declaring that she preferred to remain childless. Mother-in-law said, 'Very well. Remember that there is no deficiency on our side. Nagaraj is normal. Don't you see Gopu's wife bearing a son within two years? As the proverb goes, what can the hand that holds the plough achieve, if the hand that lifts the rice pot is unlucky?' Sita bore these taunts patiently. She had given up finally after trying other remedies, such as a forty-day penance and special pujas and then pilgrimages to remote temples. Nagaraj accepted all these suggestions sheepishly. 'If we do all that Mother suggests and yet fail to breed, nobody can blame us. We will have done our best,' he would whisper to her during their bus journey to a temple sixty miles away where the carved image of a cobra was the presiding deity and had to be anointed with milk and honey from time to time, since an astrologer had analysed from the horoscope that Sita's barrenness was due to a curse on her family, an ancestor having killed a King Cobra . . .

When Tim was five years old, Nagaraj had proposed rather timidly to his brother that he put him in school. Nagaraj feared at first that his brother might turn around and say, 'What business have you to put my son to school?' but he sounded unexpectedly mild and was not averse to the proposal. Nagaraj remarked to himself, 'I do not know how to judge Gopu. He flares up unexpectedly and also listens to reason unexpectedly as he does now – strange fellow!' Gopu just said, 'Is he not too young for school?'

'Oh, no! Stephen's take in children of three years also, very good nursery and kindergarten. Tim can enjoy the company of other children. Lots of games and playthings.'

They summoned their family priest to fix an auspicious day. Mother wanted a piper and drummer to take the boy to school in a procession after a ceremonial inauguration at home. But it was ruled out, as Stephen's was a Mission School and they might refuse admission to a child arriving in a noisy procession. So they had to be satisfied with performing the inauguration rites at home and then conduct the boy to school dressed properly, rubbing off the sandal-paste caste mark on his forehead. 'St Stephen's is no ordinary school. It was established over a century ago; its students became judges and council members and civil servants all over the country; even in England old students of St Stephen's are found . . .' Nagaraj let his imagination wax, and his brother and mother and others listened to him with interest.

Nagaraj felt victorious on the first day Tim went to school, and escorting him back and forth became his chief occupation. He accompanied Tim while he ambled down to Stephen's, stopping to watch every little object, every crow and street puppy and sparrow on the way, dawdling along. Nagaraj indulged him to the fullest, sharing his joy and wonder. They usually arrived late at the school gate – the sister in charge was tolerant towards the nursery classes. The same process was repeated when Tim was let off at four in the afternoon, once again enjoying the spectacles on the road side. Sometimes he spotted a donkey beside a wall and let out a whoop of astonishment and stood still gazing on it. Nagaraj also stood in wonderment, and when it threatened to prolong, gently pushed and piloted the youngster onward, enjoying fully every moment with Tim and through Tim.

Now Tim's coming promised to make life richer in the Kabir Street home. For his comfort, Nagaraj cleared the front room, furnished it with a table and chair, brought in a camp cot from the loft (which his brother had not noticed in the partitioning of properties). 'Boys must have beds and desks if they are to develop properly, unlike us, who read our lessons in any corner and slept in corridors, if not in cattle sheds. Our parents were indifferent. That's the reason why I am like this . . .' He paused to question his own statement. 'Like what? Nothing wrong with us. Gopu was a first class B.A. He has his defects but is a studious fellow – but he always had his room and table: I was the one shunted out hither and thither and had to do my homework in any corner available. No wonder I failed in B.A. and scraped through a third class later . . .'

After this recollection his thoughts returned to Tim's needs. He told Tim, 'Here is your room, you may shut yourself in and sit at your desk, read, read and read all day, and nobody will disturb you . . .' Next he took Tim to Albert Mission Junior College, saw his friend Jesudoss, the headmaster, and got him admitted, explaining, 'His early years were at Stephen's but his father moved to the village and his studies were interrupted . . .'

Nagaraj's mind was seething with plans for his nephew. Must consult Rajan of Rajan Cycle Mart about a bicycle for Tim and then must take him to Bari, the loquacious stationer, in order to pile on his desk paper and notebooks, and then to watch the young man in his room bent over his studies – a vision which stirred him deeply. This was an ideal place for study, absolutely silent and quiet but for his old mother's constant movement over the whole place. If the door was shut she was bound to knock on it to ask why, and not rest till it was opened. But this was a minor problem. Tim should not mind it. He was fond of his grandmother and was seen now and then sitting on her bed chatting. If he just opened the door and said he was at his studies, she was bound to feel pleased and leave him alone.

The old mother, however, did not live long enough to enjoy her grandson's company. In less than three months after his arrival she was gone. She tumbled down during her perambulation through the vast acreage of the house and was bedridden, with Tim nursing her, without leaving her side even for a moment. To cremate her, Gopu, as the elder son, came down with his family, performed the funeral rites correctly and left in a businesslike manner on the fourteenth day, hardly exchanging half a dozen words with Tim. His mother, Charu, made constant but infructuous attempts to persuade him to return home.

During those days of rituals, Nagaraj enjoyed the crowd at home, though the occasion was grim. After Gopu and family left, life became dull. Without his mother's presence, which seemed to have had the effect, unnoticed all these years, of filling all space, the house seemed to have become suddenly vast and cavernous. With Jayaraj's help, Nagaraj got a bromide enlargement of his mother made out of an early group photo, and hung it up prominently in the hall. He festooned it with flowers every morning, standing on a stool to reach it. Sita became sole mistress of the house, although suffering occasional stabs of regret at the memories of her rudeness to the old lady in recent times.

Within one year, Tim was well settled in town, and liked it. His father Gopu gradually got reconciled to the idea, and had overcome much of his bitterness against his son. However, he was not able to forgive his brother for, as he fancied, separating son from father. He thought Tim's prejudice against village life was due to Nagaraj's openly expressed aversion to the smell of cattle and cattleshed and his contempt for gobar gas, which sounded blasphemous. He said to his wife, 'Nag is absolutely ignorant. A fellow who cannot appreciate the value of gobar gas must be a bigger dunce than I take him to be. And he must have spoken slightingly of our efforts; no wonder Tim is what he is. It is our misfortune that Tim should have come under this fellow's spell. Anyway, thank God this property did not go to him. He would have reduced it to a desert within one week. Now, after all these years of labour, our farm and fields are well developed and proving profitable. We were the first to utilise the facilities government offered in the shape of pesticides and fertilisers, machinery and, above all, the gas plant. I hope we shall soon acquire tractors, too, and let our neighbours burst with envy.'

Nagaraj felt it his duty to visit the village to see the changes and improvements. 'Otherwise Gopu is likely to mistake me.' When he blurted out this sentiment, Sita just said, 'You know your brother better, and if you demean yourself it's your business. Charu will laugh at us: she is bound to tell her sisters or friends – '

Nagaraj said, 'You imagine things – I won't spend a day more than necessary. I'll come back. If I take Tim along with me, I'm sure it will change the whole picture – '

'I'd like to see you try and get Tim to go with you – '

'Why not?' he asked without any point.

'After Mother's death and their last visit,' Sita remarked at a tangent, 'your brother never cared to ask how you are, and writes only to Tim on a postcard.'

'You must not read other people's letters.'

'You don't have to tell me. One can't help reading a postcard. I look at it just to find out if he has any thought for you, while you keep thinking and talking of him all the time . . .'

Nagaraj was unequal to this kind of talk. Saying to himself, 'She is not in a good mood,' he suddenly turned round and moved off to seek asylum on the pyol. He was confident she would not follow, being busy in her world of kitchen and back yard.

He took the bus next day and visited his brother, who became excited when Nagaraj said, 'I could not stay away a minute longer after I heard from some people how the farm is transformed through your recent efforts.' This completely softened Gopu, at least for the time being. He immediately proposed to give Nagaraj a guided tour, but Charu came on the scene and said, 'First let your brother have some food. He has travelled from the town.' She turned to ask Nagaraj, 'Why has Tim not come?'

And Nagaraj said, 'He has a test and said he will come later' – while Tim had only said, 'Not interested in gobar gas, manure and garbage. Tell Mother I'll see her later.' Nagaraj had added, 'I'll also tell Gopu that you'll see him – '

'Yes,' Tim said and added, 'How can I help seeing him when I go there?'

Nagaraj was quite exhausted at the end of the guided tour. His orbit in Malgudi was limited to Kanni's shop, the Sari Centre and the river, and an occasional visit to the Town Hall library, where he used to go regularly at one time, that was before the era of Coomar's Boeing Centre. Now he terminated his outings after the morning meal at the Centre where he remained busy all day; moreover the old librarian had retired and a younger fellow was in charge, full of notions about library systems, who did not offer anyone a seat beside his desk or encourage conversation, much less show any interest in Narada. On the first day when Nagaraj introduced himself and broached the theme, he had asked, 'Are you a writer?' Nagaraj could not say yes or no, but replied, 'I live in Kabir Street.'

'I am not asking for your address. I just want to know if you are making a living as a writer.'

Nagaraj suppressed his desire to give an account of his financial status as an inheritor of ancestral wealth like other Kabir Street gentry, which was implied in his mentioning Kabir Street; he alluded to his special interest in Narada, particularly the proposed research into his ancestry. This young, forthcoming librarian dismissed the proposal instantly, 'You will not find it in this library. I am going to change all that. The shelves will be cleared of all antiquated literature. They have no relevance to our culture today. We need more literature on Five Year Plans and their effect on the welfare and economic schemes, political life and so on. India today is on the threshold of a vast social revolution . . .' Nagaraj fled from the library and gave up the habit of visiting it even occasionally. Hence, his walks were of late much reduced and his feet, unaccustomed to a lot of trudging, now ached with the inspection of the farm.

His brother had taken him through coconut groves, guava orchards, and fields where rice and millets grew; he demonstrated the technique of spraying pesticides or chemical fertilisers; he also showed him a few mechanical gadgets for threshing, for slicing and mashing cattle feeds. His masterpiece, however, was the cement gas plant. The government gave a subsidy, cement and technical staff, in order to modernise rural life. He patted the walls of the plant proudly and affectionately. Nagaraj felt he might soon bow before it, prostrate on the ground, and wave a camphor flame. Nagaraj realised that the road to the other's heart lay through the gas plant. He looked impressed with the changes although he did not understand any of it; as he could not find the right terms, he kept murmuring all through the tour, 'Wonderful! Wonderful!', so much so that Gopu said, 'Like a parrot, you are uttering the same phrase. Do you really understand anything?' Nagaraj was slightly worried how he was to come through if cross-examined. He remained silent and thoughtful. They were now in the banana grove with bunches still ripening on their stalks. The green glare from the broad leaves waving seemed to him soothing, and he declared, 'How green is this shade!'

'Banana is always green, what is there to wonder about like a baby?'

Nagaraj felt secretly that he could appreciate cabbage heaps in Malgudi market better. He could think of nothing to say except, 'Do you give it any special manure?'

'If I explain, will you understand?' Gopu asked contemptuously, moving out of the banana corner. He was rather sore that Nagaraj seemed impervious to the value of agriculture, horticulture or any culture. As they walked back home, Gopu walked ahead and Nagaraj followed with a hangdog air. Nagaraj smarted inwardly at Gopu's superciliousness, although he had seemed so enthusiastic, warm and kind at the start of the circuit when Nagaraj had feigned so much interest in the gas plant. 'One couldn't go on singing the praise of that gas god endlessly. Could one? I have gone to the maximum extent possible in appreciating his work, can't do more. Gopu is a rustic who wears a tuft and dabbles in mud and manure like a baby. He takes advantage of my silence. Suppose I turn around and face him with, "What do you know of Narada? Can you attempt a serious work which will be approved by pundits? If I am indifferent to cattle and dung, it is because I have better things on my mind."

When saying goodbye next day he felt that he owed his brother a compliment and said, 'You have done very well, especially the cement plant for gas.' As a token of goodwill, a basket of fruits and vegetables was added by Gopu to his baggage at his departure.

Nagaraj's main occupation was watching Tim's movements – unobtrusively, because he was not sure that Tim liked to be watched; so he pretended indifference and preoccupation but kept an eye on Tim from the minute he heard footsteps in his room. He rose earlier than Tim, before seven, in spite of Sita's daily effort to keep him down in bed. As we have noted, he jumped out of his bed the moment Sita was up and busy in the kitchen. He paused before Tim's door to detect the sound of movement inside. When he heard no noise, he told himself, 'The boy is still asleep, God bless him. After all, his classes begin only at ten-thirty. No hurry.' And then he went about his business but came again and again to listen at the door. When he guessed Tim was up inside, he tip-toed away. When Tim showed himself outside, Nagaraj cried, 'Had good sleep?' He ran into the kitchen to warn Sita that the young man was up and to have his coffee ready. Sita generally ignored him but sometimes replied petulantly, 'One would think you were dancing attendance on a rare son-in-law. I know he'll come in for his coffee when he wants – '

'No, no, we should not leave it like that. After all,' he drawled, unable to conclude the sentence.

'After all what?' Sita asked.

'Hush!' Nagaraj said, 'he is coming,' and did not stop to hear further comments but moved off as if he did not notice Tim. But wherever he was he seemed to possess a sort of clairvoyance and to know how Tim was sipping his coffee or asking for less sugar or milk. This was the time when the boy spent some time talking to his aunt. Nagaraj followed every word passing in the kitchen. Tim might be saying sometimes, 'I want to give up sugar.'

'Why?'

'They say it is beneficial to health to avoid it.'

'Don't you believe all that story,' Sita would say. 'Without sugar, how can you take in coffee? It is bitter.'

'Americans drink pure decoction without milk or sugar, they call it black coffee.'

'Why do they do that?'

'In order to remain slim,' would be Tim's answer.

CHAPTER 6

At ten, Nagaraj was sitting on the pyol peering into the darkness of the crossroad from the market. The boy was still away. Rather a puzzle what he was doing with himself. He had got into the habit of borrowing neighbour Sambu's scooter, imitating the Talkative Man. It was parked in the passage of Sambu's house while he was all day poring over a book beside his window. You had only to ask and the scooter was yours for the day. Sambu hardly ever stirred out of his library.

Nagaraj speculated, looking at the stars, whether Tim would have fallen off the scooter somewhere. He groaned at the thought, which brought his wife out at the door. 'What was that noise?'

'Which noise?'

'Some kind of howling.'

'I didn't notice. Perhaps a street dog howling at the moon . . .'

'Where are you? This is the dark half of the month.'

'Perhaps that's why the dog has to howl for it.'

'Why are you sitting there, to catch a cold? The boy will be back. You are too fussy. He is in college and can take care of himself – old enough.'

'That's all right, you go to bed. I like it here. It's cool . . .'

She hesitated a moment to express an opinion. 'You are not . . .' she began.

He knew what she was going to say and tried to divert her thoughts with, 'I heard today tamarind is going to be scarce – remember to buy our year's supply if it is coming in basket headloads from villages.'

'Available in plenty. Why do you worry about it now?'

'Because they are exporting lorry loads to Iraq . . .'

She laughed at the notion, 'Iraq? Where is it? Do they also eat rasam and sambhar? Their food would be different.'

'I only told you what I have heard.'

She burst into a laugh. 'In your Sari Centre you seem to hear strange reports.'

Further talk was not possible as the scooter was heard coming at the market end of the lane. Nagaraj wished he could find more time for a discussion with his nephew and demand an explanation, but it seemed impossible. From the minute he got up from bed the young man moved up and down the house and then constantly went out on his bicycle or the neighbour's scooter, and returned home late. Sita did not share her husband's blind leniency towards the boy. She felt at times that he would benefit by a sound thrashing. She found it impossible to depend on his words. He was full of charm but never meant what he said, and proved slippery. He would promise to be on time for food but could never be found when others were ready and waiting. He would pick up his college books and bicycle, open the front door and just vanish while she and her husband were before their plates in the dining room. Why he behaved thus could not be understood. Till he was expected in the kitchen, he would be hanging about his aunt uttering pleasantries and sometimes also detailing his preference in food matters, and then suddenly disappear. Nagaraj, though puzzled by his behaviour, would explain it away. 'He'll be back – must have thought of something suddenly about his college and will come back . . .'

When he was in, it was impossible to get angry with him. He displayed such friendliness and dogged his aunt's footsteps in the vast house, talking and explaining to her scientific wonders, world events and all kinds of things. He would ask, 'What is the menu today?' and express his joy at whatever he heard, only to disappear when they were getting ready to serve him. But not every time. Sometimes he stayed on and expressed appreciation of his aunt's culinary genius. That pleased her greatly, but only for the time being. She had misgivings about him sometimes, rather bewildered by his manner. On some evenings he would appear unexpectedly at an odd hour and say plaintively, 'I'm dying of hunger. Give me anything.' The lady would feel so pleased that she would bustle about and feed him. Soon after eating he would take his bicycle or the neighbour's scooter and disappear, much to the bewilderment of Nagaraj while he was planning a quiet chat with him on the pyol.

Today, when the boy passed in, Nagaraj sniffed. He detected a faint alcohol flavour in the air. That disturbed his mind for a moment. He wondered if the young fellow was out somewhere sitting up in evil company. The Talkative Man had mentioned some time ago that he had noticed his nephew in a group of young men at Kismet in New Extension. Nagaraj felt disturbed but covered it up quickly. He wanted to ask if Kismet was such a horrible place that one should not be seen there, but the Talkative Man, as ever in a hurry, did not stop to explain. Nagaraj asked him later, 'What is Kismet?'

'A sort of club and restaurant and bar – started by a North Indian – very popular and fashionable.'

'What do they have there?'

'Anything from ice cream to whisky and soda, and dinner if ordered – '

'Oh, whisky!' Horrible word, not for Kabir Street families, in spite of the engineer in the last house who tottered about muttering imprecations and challenges every evening, abandoned by his family who had left him and moved out of town.

'Do you go there every day?' Nagaraj asked, his curiosity increasing every moment.

'Not every day; sometimes to meet people – it's something new to us in Malgudi.'

Nagaraj left it at that, worrying secretly why Tim should be seen there. Very uneasy thoughts followed. When Tim passed leaving a trail of alcoholic scent, Nagaraj began to sniff every day and felt relieved when he did not detect the smell. However, one evening he could not help asking, 'I find some sort of smell when you pass, something like a spirit stove of a doctor's . . .'

Tim laughed and explained, 'Oh, that! How well you remember old scents, though spirit stoves are abandoned nowadays!'

Nagaraj followed the boy into the passage and could not rest until he got an explanation about it.

Tim explained, 'Some chap sprayed eau-de-Cologne on me.'

'Why?'

'They play that sort of joke in our club.'

'But your breath also smells when you talk.'

'Oh, that chap sprayed it on my lips too . . .'

CHAPTER 7

Worry had been a luxury unknown to Nagaraj till now. Nowadays when he sat on the pyol he realised that his mind had lost its poise. His thoughts constantly revolved round the subject of Tim, with many questions unanswered, and he found it exhausting.

Formerly when he sat down cross-legged on the pyol he could watch tranquilly the scenes in the street: not only the men, women and pedlars but also the swarm of sparrows at the rice mill, the school of crows on the roof of the house opposite and, above all, glimpses of a pedigreed white terrier with brown patches around the eyes next door, imported from Singapore, who had his outing on a leash only when the family went out. He was always well groomed and brushed and sheltered comfortably; he had never known the company of other dogs and lived in luxury. But his owners made the mistake of building a mansion in New Extension and the pedigreed terrier did not like the idea: when the affluent family moved, the dog was also led away but he sprang back to Kabir Street, breaking out of his fancy kennel in New Extension within a couple of days. He curled up happily in the road dust in Kabir Street in front of the abandoned house, when he was not trotting in the company of ruffianly mongrels behind any bitch within sight. He apparently preferred vagrancy to a sheltered aristocratic existence, flourishing on scraps and leftovers found in garbage heaps and enjoying the thrill of street fights with intruding dogs. He was bitten and scarred, and became almost unrecognisable as the tramphood developed, his coat turning yellow with grime. Not all the blandishments and efforts of his owners to rehabilitate him were of any avail. Presently one noticed here and there in Kabir Street white puppies with brown patches. All of which reminded Nagaraj of a Tamil verse his grandmother had taught him: 'House the dog in a cage, groom him, splash on him turmeric and perfume, yet you cannot uplift him – underneath it all he will remain a dog.'

While formerly Nagaraj could watch this canine tramp with detachment, philosophising about him, finding a similarity with certain human beings who gave up worldly pleasures and ties for a life of wandering as scholars or saints, nowadays the sight of that vagrant terrier stirred up uneasy feelings about Tim. Was he rolling in dust and fighting others, driven by the same impulse as moved the terrier? He had preferred Kabir Street to his village, and now went farther, even abandoning Kabir Street to some mysterious existence, coming home late smelling of eau-de-Cologne. He laughed at the notion of eau-de-Cologne. Did the boy take him to be an idiot? Just because he was old-fashioned and moved about in dhoti and shirt and upper cloth instead of pants and bush-shirt? Had he not known drinking people in his day? Coomar, who in his youth could outdo all the eau-de-Cologne spraying folk in the world! He laughed at the naiveté of his nephew, who took him to be an unobservant fool.

When he was reflecting thus, Sita came out for some minor marketing at the corner shop and stopped short on hearing Nagaraj's laughter. 'What is going on?' she asked, surprised. 'Are you talking to yourself?'

'Why not?' Nagaraj asked. 'I am my best listener: quiet and agreeable and never disputing.'

'One would take you for a crackpot.'

'Why not? People are more tolerant of crackpots.'

'You go on saying "why not" for everything. It's becoming difficult to talk to you nowadays.'

'No such complaint from my side,' he said, and she turned away in exasperation and went down the street.

Nagaraj resumed his speculations about Tim. 'It might after all be actual eau-de-Cologne – such pranks were likely but rather costly; who pays for it?' He pulled his mind back from the theme with an effort. 'After all, Tim smelled of eau-de-Cologne only occasionally – unfair to stick it to him. I am probably exaggerating and misapprehending, bloating the theme by too much brooding. I'm becoming more and more critical of the young man with the soft down on his upper lip, eyes open in perpetual wonder, the same as it used to be when going to St Stephen's. In those days he gaped at any insect or animal which came to his notice – nowadays probably there are other things. Poor boy, trusts in my trust in him. I'm betraying him by this kind of thinking – must not allow this trend. If Sita suspected I harboured suspicion about Tim, God alone knows what she would do. She might fight me, being so fond of him. On the other hand, she might agree with my own evil notions and turn hostile and create difficulties for the boy until he fled to his father in the village, realising that it was the lesser of the two evils.'

Nagaraj's heart bled at the hostile notions that were seething in his head about the young fellow, who came and went unsuspecting of his uncle's devious, evil notions – all because he stayed away late and brought in a whiff of eau-de-Cologne occasionally. And it would be a sin to draw a parallel between the trusting child who had sought asylum here and that truant dog lying in the road dust. He was appalled at the thought of his own perfidy. All because of lack of proper occupation – except when he was at the Sari Centre. Must attend to that work more seriously and not take advantage of Coomar's tolerance by leaving the Sari Centre before closing hours. Must also start on Narada soon. Pray to Narada to guide him. But Narada was not a god, he was only a sage with divine powers. No one heard of a prayer to Narada; nowhere in the scriptures did one ever come across any prayer supplicating, 'O Narada . . .'

These days Nagaraj never waited for Tim but had his supper at his normal hour. Sita, too, held out for some time, saying, 'I'll wait for Tim. It does not look proper . . .' After realising that Tim came home only after ten or eleven in the night, she stopped waiting for him and joined Nagaraj at supper, and filled a couple of bowls with rice and vegetables for Tim to help himself to whenever he should come home.

Sitting in the hall they discussed the subject (Tim) at night when the after-dinner calmness had descended on the house. 'What does he do so late in this town?' they asked each other untiringly every night.

'Why not ask him straight away?' she said.

'I don't get a chance. I see only flashes of him before he picks up his bicycle and leaves – I can't hold him for a talk.'

She said, 'You haven't tried. You are his uncle and guardian, you have a responsibility. Your brother can come down on you any time if he finds you are neglecting duty.'

'That's true, you are right,' Nagaraj said ruefully. 'But I don't know . . . What do you think I should do?'

'You must be a little more firm,' she said. 'Why do you quail in his presence?'

'Why don't you ask him yourself? You have been more than a mother to him.'

She rejected the idea and simply said, 'It's a man's job.'

'How do you want me to set about it?'

'As soon as you see him first thing in the morning, tell him, "Don't go away. I want to talk to you," and then get him to sit down with you on this bench or in my room, and take care not to go to the pyol for this meeting, where the whole street will be listening – '

'But in his room, there is only one chair,' Nagaraj said dolefully. 'I can't keep him standing and lecture to him like a school teacher.'

'In that case, this hall bench should do. I promise I'll keep away in the kitchen so as to leave you both alone.'

Nagaraj did not like the idea; he felt he could not face his nephew alone. 'No, you must also be there. It's better two of us talk to him, rather than one,' he told his wife, feeling that an impossible duty was being thrust on him and wishing he could don the ochre robe and go into silence for ever. At the sound of the bicycle being lifted up the front steps, they became alert. Sita ran to the door and Tim entered with a smile, and at that smile all their misgivings vanished, and she deliberately avoided sniffing the air for liquor. 'It is not fair to suspect him.' Nagaraj rose from the bench, cheerily asking, 'Had a good day, Tim? Your dinner is ready.'

The boy just said, 'I'll change and come,' and went to his room.

Next evening they started worrying about him again, and Nagaraj decided, 'Tomorrow or the day after, I'll talk to him . . .' While Tim departed and arrived as usual, without bothering about them, a postcard from the village arrived and created uneasiness. Nagaraj found it under the street door and could not help perusing it. The card, from Gopu, said, 'Boy, what is happening? You never write, and we do not know whether you are studying or wasting your time. If your uncle thinks he can leave you to live the existence of an unleashed donkey, he is mistaken. I'll make him answer for your deeds . . .' And so on, a long letter in pin-point writing, loading on the poor postcard enough words to cover four sheets of notepaper. 'The miser!' Nagaraj muttered to himself, 'why can't he use a large sheet of paper and envelope instead of using a postcard for his epic-length message? If he wrote it properly and sent it sealed, I wouldn't know what he was thinking. However, thank God for the postcard. I know Gopu's mind now . . .'

He somehow wished to avoid mentioning this card to Sita, and quietly took it and left it on Tim's table. 'Food for thought in that postcard. Yes, Sita once again has shown that her premonitions were sound. Must be guided by her advice again in all matters. Didn't she warn me about my brother coming down on me for neglecting Tim? Must talk to Tim as advised by Sita.' But she would not participate in that exercise, and by himself he would not achieve anything. Anyway, he would try to talk to him and not let him go on like an unleashed donkey. 'Gopu was truly ungrateful and ungracious. I must follow Sita's strategy to corner Tim first thing in the day, assuming a tone of authority and firmness.' He rehearsed the scene for a while.

Next morning, he felt feverish sitting on the hall bench, watching and waiting for Tim's door to open. Sita kept an eye on him. She constantly came out of the kitchen with a significant glance in his direction, and passed up and down in front of him, hissing as she passed, 'After the card from your brother, you must act, otherwise . . .'

'We should not have read his card, that's why I placed it on his table. Why did you read it?'

'Have I no right to go into his room?' she asked angrily in whispers. Nagaraj was trying to frame a fitting reply when she cut in with, 'Hush, I hear him moving . . .' in a conspiratorial tone.

Nagaraj asked mentally, 'What on earth do you expect me to do?' She went back into the kitchen and Nagaraj felt more lost than ever, wishing that she had stayed on to lend him support in confronting Tim, who had not emerged yet from his room. Nagaraj felt a brief reprieve, it seemed, from a harsh sentence. If Sita could lend her voice and fill up the pauses and gaps in his own proposed dialogue with Tim, that would be a great help.

While he was brooding thus, Sita made a dash from the kitchen again, to whisper, 'Be firm and clear. After your brother's postcard, it is your duty . . .' 'How', he wanted to ask, but she turned round and retreated into the kitchen in a flash, as if afraid to be seen in his company. 'Why is she avoiding me?' Nagaraj thought. 'After all, we are lawfully wedded . . .' He wanted to go and tell her firmly, 'You were not expected to read his letter.' But she had taken refuge in the kitchen in a cowardly manner after handing him the dagger. From some unplumbed depths of memory he thought of the dagger scene from *Macbeth*, which he had studied for his B.A. examination, in a previous incarnation as it seemed. Lady Macbeth, egging her husband on to stab the sleeping king . . . Macbeth had a less difficult job, as he had only to tackle a sleeping king, not a moving target like Tim. Actually Sita was acting more like Narada: creating complications between two parties (himself and Tim).

Following this idea, Nagaraj was happily lost in plans for his magnum opus on Narada, till the door opened and Tim appeared; at the sight of him, fresh from sleep, with his crop ruffled, all the well-rehearsed lines were gone. Tim didn't give him any chance either. He threw a glance at his uncle and swiftly moved off to the bath at the back yard. Nagaraj didn't know what to do now. He felt he had failed in his duty and had let down Sita. She was bound to attack him for his hesitancy. His opening lines would have been, as soon as Tim appeared at the door, 'Tim, don't go away before I have a word with you,' in a firm, unambiguous tone. But one can't fling such a sentence at another just waking up – as bad as stabbing a sleeping king. One should allow a decent margin of time for such things. But Sita was unrealistic and impetuous. Thank God she did not expect him to bawl at Tim's bedside, 'I must have a word with you!'

Half an hour later Tim was returning to his room, after a wash and coffee. He showed surprise at finding his uncle in the hall at this time, when normally he should be out at Jayaraj's or on the pyol to observe the street life in the morning. 'Not gone out, Uncle?' he asked.

This would have been the right cue for his rehearsed sentence, 'I'm only waiting for you, don't go away, etc.' But Nagaraj could only say, 'Just for a change, that's all, I'll start out later, perhaps . . .' As he was hesitating, the boy was gone. He did not wait for Nagaraj to spin out his sentence. He went into his room, shutting the door behind him, while Nagaraj kept gazing on it not knowing what to do next, dreading lest Sita should come before him again with her sinister looks and hissing commands. Presently she did come out to ask, 'Have you . . . ?'

In sheer desperation he nodded 'yes'. It was a lie, of course, but a life-saving one as it seemed to him. She asked him in the same undertone, 'What did he say?'

'Don't ask now, I'll tell everything later,' with an air of deep diplomacy. While she was trying to say something, he said in a tone of urgency, 'Begone, here he cometh . . .' feeling vaguely indebted to Shakespeare again though he had lost his own lines ordered by Sita.

He felt victorious when she left him alone: he had achieved grand results this morning. He thought that he now understood the importance of tact and diplomacy in domestic life. 'Ninety-nine per cent of husbands must be practising diplomacy for survival since wives were all alike, thoughtless and commanding. If men weren't crafty, family structure would have crumbled long ago. The greatness of our society lies in its stability, unlike the West, where one reads of divorces . . .' The boy came out dressed in pants and a white shirt. 'Never wears a dhoti,' Nagaraj commented mentally, 'Nothing wrong with dhoti, but these boys are imitating Western fashions . . .' He felt vaguely bound to greet Tim and establish communion, so he said, 'Going out so soon?'

'Yes,' said the boy, moving towards his bicycle on its stand at the front door.

'What about food?'

'I'll be back . . .' That was his usual answer. Some days he came back, often he didn't. Nagaraj said in an undertone, 'Your aunt will have food ready by nine.'

'I will come back and eat,' repeated Tim in a flat voice.

Nagaraj would have asked next, had he a chance, 'What is the hurry?' and would have gone on smoothly to speak his lines, 'Don't go away, I must speak to you.' But the boy did not give him a chance, he reached his bicycle, took it off its stand, opened the front door and was gone. At least he had been planning an opening gambit, with, 'Let me come to the door and see you off . . .' but he did not get a chance. He knew Sita was keeping a secret watch on him but he defeated her by talking to Tim under his breath so that Sita should hear nothing but infer from appearances that some serious talk was going on.

After Tim was gone, Nagaraj moved on to his pyol seat, without going in to report to Sita the substance of his talk with the nephew. 'Good to leave her guessing till she comes out.' Sita was busy cooking and could not leave the kitchen; she had been straining her ears to catch the drift of her husband's conversation with Tim, but it was inaudible – they had been talking in an unusually low key. She could only distinguish two voices overlapping each other: her husband's phlegmatic rambling and the gruff tone of Tim. Unable to contain her curiosity, the moment the rice was ready to be lifted off the fire, she left the kitchen and sought out Nagaraj on the pyol. She stood at the door and summoned him to come in. 'Why?' he asked.

'Wish to know what happened. We can't talk there, you know it.'

He was sitting on the platform with his knees drawn up and legs crossed comfortably as in a yoga pose, and was reluctant to uncoil himself but she stood there unrelenting. He was about to say something, but she ordered peremptorily, 'Please be good enough to get up and step in.' He obliged her by crossing the threshold and advancing a few inches, wondering what to say; he was still in the glow of a discovery, namely the unimportance of a direct answer and the peace that comes consequently. But he realised at the same time that the tactic should be adopted with circumspection, otherwise it might lead to disaster. While his mind was thrashing out this question she stood there impatiently, waiting for his report. 'Have you nothing to say?' she asked with forced moderation. 'The kettle is on, I've to get back.'

'What for?' he asked inanely.

She ignored his question and straight away asked, 'What did he say?'

'Well, one wouldn't expect him to say anything, what one had to tell him being more important.'

'Did he listen?'

'Yes, of course, he had to, otherwise . . .'

He sounded so menacing that Sita felt pleased and said, 'I'm glad you are stirring yourself after all.'

'Naturally! You don't understand me. Rome was not built in a day . . .' he suddenly said, another literary tag welling up from some unsuspected depth.

She said, 'Who cares about Rome?' rather taken aback by his sudden dash to Rome. 'What had he to say?' she persisted.

'We should wait and not rush him. I have my own way of managing all situations, as you well know.' He got into a mood of victorious self-analysis, but Sita had no patience to stand there and listen. She turned to go, asking again, 'What did he have to say?'

Nagaraj replied, 'What can he say, after the way I spoke to him? But he is very shrewd. He'll have understood how one feels though he didn't show it . . .'

Apparently Sita was pleased with his answers and left muttering, 'I cannot afford to lounge on the pyol, I have things to do . . .'

CHAPTER 8

Thinking it over, Nagaraj realised that he had achieved nothing; the problem of Tim remained where it began, although he had appeased Sita. 'Gopu has called his son an unleashed donkey, a thoroughly wrong notion, which shows Gopu knows nothing about donkeys,' he said to himself. 'In the village probably donkeys are found all over the place unless tethered, but here, in an orderly town like Malgudi, they conduct themselves admirably.' He noticed the Kabir Street donkeys, numbering four, always stood like statues beside a blank wall, which was the back of a house opening on the other side of a lane. They belonged to the washermen living in huts, who loaded their backs with soiled clothes collected from the neighbourhood and whipped them on towards the river where they would do their laundering. When they came back from the river, the animals were unleashed, but they always remained standing in a meditative pose and never moved except to chew an old newspaper or a dining leaf blown by the wind in their direction. They occasionally let out a thundering bray in unison, to relieve the tedium perhaps – but move? Never.

'What did Gopu mean by talking about an unleashed donkey loafing about and likening it to Tim? Must be rather hurting to a young soul. Wonder how he could swallow that kind of insult written on a postcard! He was probably used to being called an unleashed donkey by his father, but at some stage rebelled and came here to live with us. I'm honoured to have his trust in me – good boy, so decent in his behaviour, not a day was he ever rude or impertinent. Why should he be rude when we are so gentle with him? Sita never showed any diminution of her love (from the day he came as a three-month-old baby), although she wants me to control him firmly, finding his ways rather puzzling. She wants to know where he goes and spends his time, what has happened to his college studies? It's all, of course, very important, indeed it's my duty to find out. No wonder Gopu threatens to come down on me and hold me responsible. When did I last visit Albert Mission?' It seemed a decade ago.

Even when he came face to face with Professor Jesudoss at the market the other day, it never occurred to him to make any enquiry about the young fellow. After a cursory salutation and some formal remarks about the price of commodities in the market, they parted. The reason why he had to hurry away was that they had met in front of the fish stall and he could not stand the stink, although Jesudoss did not seem to mind it; perhaps he was taking a fish home in his plastic shopping bag. Nagaraj pulled his mind back to Tim. He decided to concentrate on him and not let other thoughts intrude. First thing was to find out whether Tim was attending his classes.

At three in the afternoon, after closing his account book at the Sari Centre, he went up to Coomar to say, 'The Public Prosecutor's account is overdue.'

'We may have to wait a little longer,' said Coomar, looking up from yarn samples he had been examining.

'No,' said Nagaraj, 'don't allow too much time, the marriage took place over a year ago.'

'Nag, give me a couple of weeks more and if they don't respond we'll take whatever steps may be necessary,' said Coomar.

Nagaraj said, as if conceding a point, 'Very well, but don't let it get out of hand.' He felt he had offered sound advice though, if Coomar had asked him to specify the steps to take he would have felt uncomfortable. He would perhaps have suggested that his family lawyer, who was now in dotage, serve a notice on the Public Prosecutor. But would a declining lawyer ever have the guts to challenge a Public Prosecutor to settle a sari account? He concluded they were all of the same gang, including Coomar. 'Who knows?' He said to Coomar, 'I'll see you tomorrow. I've some work now,' making a move. He went down Market Road, saw an autorickshaw in front of the City Hardware Store. He was about to summon it when Gupta, the owner of Hardware, hailed him from his seat inside the shop.

'Nagaraj, why don't you come in? Come and have tea and then go. What have you been doing with yourself all these days?'

'I have to go to Albert Mission before it closes.'

'Have you become a student again? Ha, ha!'

Nagaraj shouted back from the street, 'I have my nephew studying there . . .

'Oh! Come in, come in. Is he your nephew Tom?'

'No, Tim,' corrected Nagaraj, feeling outraged. They named dogs Tom.

'Yes, yes, sorry for the mistake. My hearing is not at all good these days. Come in for a minute and have a cup of coffee – excellent coffee from New Udupi next door.'

Nagaraj stepped in, reflecting, 'Offered tea, and now coffee! What is he going to give me, really?'

Gupta, the owner of Hardware, seated him on a stool across his table and ordered his servant to fetch coffee with the warning, 'Must be the best coffee, otherwise tell that man I'll pay him off and open my account at Anand.' He explained, 'Malgudi is not what it used to be a couple of years ago – so much competition in every trade.' Sipping his coffee, Nagaraj heard Gupta say, 'Tom is here sometimes – '

'Tim,' corrected Nagaraj.

'Yes, yes, sorry. Timmy comes here – '

'Not Timmy, but Tim,' corrected Nagaraj again, feeling outraged and saying to himself, 'What a fellow! Cannot remember a simple name.'

'What is the meaning of Tim?' asked Gupta irrelevantly.

'Deity in our village temple,' replied Nagaraj on an inspiration.

'What god is that?' asked Gupta with curiosity. Nagaraj gave some answer describing the image as possessing four arms and three eyes.

'Oh!' said Gupta, impressed. 'It must be an aspect of Siva. You must get me a photo for my collection. My walls at home are covered with photographs of gods in their hundreds. I ask for a photograph from any friend who mentions a new god.'

'Very good habit,' Nagaraj commented. 'Nobler than collecting portraits of film stars.'

Gupta confessed, 'Would you believe it? I never see films.'

'I used to see a lot in my youth, yes, even the cinema posters I don't look at now.' How Tim came to be known here bothered Nagaraj but he did not want to talk about him, and looked as if it were the most natural thing for Tim's name to be heard in a hardware shop.

He stood up, saying, 'I must see Jesudoss at Albert Mission before it closes . . .' and hurried out lest he should hear something shocking about Tim if he lingered. The autorickshaw was still there. He got into it and ordered, 'Albert Mission before closing time.'

The driver said, 'Rather far off – you must give me more.'

'More than what?'

'More than what the meter shows – if we get paid according to the meter, we will have to starve, considering the petrol price.'

'But I don't see a meter in your vehicle.'

'There are some vehicles with meters, but the police have . . .' He went on with his rambling account of the problems of running an autorickshaw service. Nagaraj stamped his foot and said, 'Are you going to start or not? I've to go to Albert Mission before their closing time.'

'It's beyond the level crossing.'

'I didn't build the college, whichever side of the level crossing it may happen to be,' said Nagaraj.

'Extra for points beyond level crossing.'

Gupta happened to watch the scene from his seat, and shouted, 'Why are you haggling with my friend? Get going, Muni.'

At this the rickshaw-man said, 'He is the boss and I must obey him. If he interferes and loses, it's his business. I don't care. Do I wait at the school and bring you back?'

'Yes, I live in Kabir Street.'

With all his dallying it was late when Nagaraj reached the college. But Jesudoss was still in his room. They were old friends and could chat for half an hour. Nagaraj did not want to show that he was spying on Tim. He had to conceal his intention and worries and also find out the whereabouts of his nephew, whom he had wildly hoped to meet at Albert Mission. In the midst of their talks, Jesudoss asked suddenly, 'Why have you stopped Krishnaji?'

'We call him Tim.'

'Doesn't matter what you call him, but what is he doing?'

Nagaraj was at his wits' end to find an answer while covering up his shock. It would have been easier if he could have afforded to be frank. But his desire to protect Tim was overwhelming. He feared that if he spoke plainly he might have to blurt out his brother's phrase, 'unleashed donkey'. So he gave no direct answer to Jesudoss but just said, 'Oh, as a teacher you must have noticed how young men want to try new experiments and carve careers for themselves.'

'All very well, but education should come first. Krishnaji was a bright student and I went out of my way to give him admission, and you withdrew him even without a word to me!'

Nagaraj felt cowed by his tone and flashing eyes and said, 'I have come now exactly for that purpose!'

'After a whole term?' Jesudoss said cynically, pulling out a register, opening a page and thrusting it forth, with his finger stabbing a line. 'He came first at the last term test!'

'I told you he is a clever boy, above average.'

'And yet you would not force him to continue his studies!' said Jesudoss accusingly.

Nagaraj began to feel guilty. The need to be on the defensive (not really knowing what he was defending) was fatiguing. When he met Jesudoss outside, at the fish market, for instance, the Professor was so mild and friendly. But in his official seat within the four walls of Albert Mission, he sounded terrible. How people assumed different avatars on different occasions, he marvelled secretly. He had always viewed Jesudoss as his best friend, never as a prosecutor. He was now displaying an aspect which was shocking. Nagaraj regretted coming out here at all, blamed his brother's postcard and Sita for his predicament, and sat wondering how to terminate the interview. At this point, Jesudoss himself rose, saying, 'We call them "drop-outs" and know fully how helpless parents or guardians can be anyway . . .'

Nagaraj fled to his autorickshaw, reflecting, 'I had thought of him as an easy-going friend, what a mistake!'

CHAPTER 9

Nagaraj fell into an introspective state of mind that evening while he sat on the pyol and watched the stars. Sita noticed that he was unusually moody and silent. Normally, as soon as he came home for the day, he would have a wash, change his dress, and go into the puja room for half a second, stand before the gods with his eyes shut, pick up a small pinch of sacred ash from the wooden bowl, press it on his brow, and then call Sita and ask for something to eat and drink, and enjoy the usual banter with her. But today his pattern of behaviour changed, much to Sita's puzzlement. First, he was late coming home. He flung off his uppercloth and shirt and did not stop to ask for coffee but repaired to his pyol and sat brooding.

Sita felt disturbed, having mostly known him as vivacious and talkative. Now his silence seemed unnatural. The only other occasion on which he remained moody was when his mother was laid up, years ago, with a fractured hip; and another time, earlier, when Tim was carried away in the tempo van on the day the brothers separated. Of course, other occasions were minor ones when they had arguments on domestic matters. But today, thinking back, Sita felt she had done nothing to upset him. In her turn she became introspective while cutting some vegetables for dinner. She was so preoccupied that she hurt her finger, and a drop of blood oozed out. She came out of the kitchen holding up her finger and asked Nagaraj, 'Have you got a plaster or something? I have cut my finger.' At the sight of her bleeding finger, Nagaraj let out a shriek which brought the lady next door to ask, 'What has happened?' Nagaraj wailed, 'Oh! She has cut her finger . . .'

'Just a scratch, that's all. Have you any plaster or ointment? We have nothing in this house,' said Sita.

'I have everything,' said the lady. 'With all the children in the house, one has to keep these things.' She led Sita into her house and stuck a plaster on the hurt finger, Nagaraj trailing behind her anxiously, uttering cries of sympathy. When they were coming back, he asked, 'How did it happen?'

She whispered, 'Please don't go to the pyol and mope again. Come into the house – otherwise that lady will not miss a word of our talk. Shut the door and come in.'

'Do you feel any pain?' he asked solicitously.

'It's just a scratch, I tell you. You didn't even come for coffee. What's the matter?' He followed her into the kitchen and sat down on a plank, which pleased Sita. She busied herself scrubbing some utensils and putting them back on a shelf.

'If you make less noise with all those clanging vessels, you can hear me say something interesting.'

Her curiosity was aroused. She said, 'Wait till I have done with these vessels. Go and wait in the hall. Whether my finger bleeds or not, I alone have to do things in this house. No one else . . . Now go. I'll be with you in ten minutes.' Her manner was unusually mild; he felt happy she was showing so much concern for his moods. He said, 'No, I'll stay here. Give me a little buttermilk with salt and a squeeze of lime and a dash of asafoetida in it – just the thing for the hot day. Make it thin.' He enjoyed the fuss and affability Sita displayed, and thought that she probably guessed the turbulence in his mind. The buttermilk made him cool and composed, and he said suddenly, 'Sita, listen.' She turned her head slightly from the oven, frying something, and said, 'I'm listening.'

He sat blinking, and toyed with the thought, 'If I pick up my ochre dress, I could remain dumb and Sita won't know a thing.' He was worried how she might react to his news about Tim. She was so devoted to him that she might fall into a fit and froth at the mouth; he might have to call again the lady next door for help, as he had no idea whatever how to handle such a situation. 'Better not tell her anything now,' he decided, but Sita came up and sat beside him on another plank. 'We are like newlyweds; actually these two sitting planks came from your father on the day of our wedding,' said Nagaraj.

'Why do you have to tell me that now? Don't I remember how your father behaved at the time? He insisted on rose-wood planks with silver studs at the corners and shouted and lost his temper when he found that the silver studs were rather tiny. My father looked panic-stricken and got a silversmith immediately to make and fix these roses in the corners . . .'

After this digression, she drew her plank closer and said, 'Now go on. I know it is Tim.'

He was taken aback. 'You are uncanny,' he cried. 'How did you guess?'

'What else would you be thinking of? Now tell me. I'm glad you are becoming active about that boy after all. It would have been so good if you had listened to me and acted earlier.'

'Why bother about all that now?' he said, feeling happy that she wasn't giving him any chance to open his mouth. He felt shielded by her garrulity and monologue, and felt he was being given a chance indeed to choose the right phrase to convey the shocking news about Tim. She was bound to turn round and accuse him again of neglecting his duty as an uncle. The important thing was to convey the news properly so that it didn't recoil on him. He was searching, like a writer in the throes of composition, for the precise sentence and the right emphasis. As he sat cogitating, she said with a smile, 'If you want to hide something – don't.'

'Don't what?' he asked, to mark time without having to come to the point. She was very patient and considerate and did not hustle him but humoured him throughout and waited patiently until he told her about Tim's dropping out of school. When he blurted it out, in his own way, he felt relieved, a great burden off his chest. And she said, 'We must decide what to do next.'

They discussed Tim but could come to no decision about the next step.

'Shall I visit my brother and tell him the facts?'

'What facts have you got?' asked Sita.

Nagaraj said, 'That Tim has dropped out.'

'If he asks in his usual style what you were doing all these days before discovering it . . . ?'

Nagaraj had no answer. He made some gurgling noise at the throat and she said, 'Will that be your answer?' with a wicked gleam in her eyes. Nagaraj felt she should not heckle him but resume the considerate, gentle manner she had shown a little while ago when he was moody. He wished he could assume the same mood again but found it impossible. Once he had got the matter off his chest, he felt light and cheerful, and he appealed, 'Please help me. Don't go on like this.' She said firmly, 'We must send Tim back to his father if he is not studying. There can be no excuse for holding him back here.'

'No one is holding him back. He is here out of his own free will.'

'Well try and tell your brother so; let us see what he says.' He appealed again. 'Sita, don't let us be lost in lectures and discussions. Tell me what to do. Help me with your advice. You are gifted . . .'

That compliment won her and she said, 'Let us hear what Tim has to say.'

That seemed such a sensible way out of this problem that he cried, 'Excellent idea, absolutely first class!' and he tapped his head and said, 'Surprised why it didn't occur here.'

Later they sat down to their supper with a sense of relief,

feeling that they had found a master key for all problems. That mood lasted till Tim arrived at his usual hour and went about cheerfully demanding, 'Auntie, food, please.' They waited until he finished eating and came back to the hall. Sita joined them in the hall after shutting the kitchen for the day, looking too serious. Tim, who was unusually jovial today, remarked, 'Auntie, thinking of something? Won't you tell me what?' She looked at Nagaraj to open the subject, but he was confused and prayed that Sita would provide the opening lines. She, however, remained dumb – only by her look she tried to goad Nagaraj on. Tim looked from one to the other. Nagaraj cleared his throat and asked, 'How is Albert Mission these days?'

'Must be as bad as ever,' he replied, and added, 'Who knows?'

'Surely, you must know!'

'No,' replied Tim briefly, got up suddenly and said, 'I got a prize in a lottery.'

'How much?' they could not help asking in a chorus.

'Not much, but I share it with a friend,' he said.

'Won't you explain how much you got?'

'I won't know my share yet, some friends are taking care of it.'

'You said "a friend".'

'Did I? My mistake,' and he laughed.

'Where is the ticket?'

'Not with me, otherwise I would have come with sweets for you – Oh, Kismet sweets are so good!'

Nagaraj looked at Sita and simultaneously they came to the conclusion that something was wrong somewhere. Tim suddenly got up and shut himself in his room. Nagaraj felt like banging his fist on the door to get Tim out. But all that he could do was to pace the hall up and down, sunk in thought. Sita left him with a significant glance at the door and retired to the bedroom. Nagaraj would have preferred to go out on to the pyol, peer into the silent dark street, and clarify his thoughts, but Sita had bolted and barred the massive door, and would object to its being opened, and it could not be opened without its ancient hinges creaking. When he went to bed, Sita asked, 'What do you make of it all?'

'Don't take him seriously, he is joking, that's all.'

She ordered, 'Tomorrow you must take the first bus to the village and tell your brother. It's your duty.'

'What is there to tell Gopu? There is nothing to say.'

'Tim seems to have come home drunk today.'

'I sniffed, but did not smell anything.'

'You don't smell anything because you don't want to. We cannot go on like this . . . It's all wrong. Are you going to talk to your brother or not?'

She looked so firm and determined that he felt like crying out, 'Oh, Lady Macbeth again!' To add to his discomfiture, she added, 'First talk to Tim, and then go to the village and discuss this matter like two normal human beings. It is very serious.' She added, 'If you are not going, I'll myself go, first thing in the morning.'

'Oh! Macbeth!' he felt like crying out, and spent an uneasy night, unable to sleep. He kept questioning again and again, 'Why is she taking such a dreadfully serious view of things while we don't know what he means by "lottery" and "share" and "friends"? We don't have the patience to wait and ask questions but must rush and make it worse. The boy looked unusually cheerful until his mood was spoilt by cross-examination. Who knows the full truth? Perhaps he has a bumper prize, which even as a share might be substantial – these are days when lottery prizes amount to fifty lakhs. Even a share will make Tim rich. What would he do with it?'

Nagaraj's mind conjured up visions of Tim's affluence, and that was very pleasant until he remembered Sita's command to him to leave for the village. Otherwise she threatened to go herself. What are women coming to these days, ordering men about!

Gopu with his wife arrived suddenly next morning. Nagaraj fell into a confused state of mind. As he greeted and received them his mind kept drumming the thought, 'Thank God Sita's scheming to despatch me to the village is dropped now, or will she still insist on driving me to the village even while they are here? Anything is likely with Sita . . .'

There was a great deal of fussing and hospitality and no explanation asked for the visits, or surprise shown, as they might offend the visitors. Sita displayed undiluted ecstasy on meeting her sister-in-law after such a long time. The hubbub of their greetings woke up Tim, who emerged from his room confused and half sleepy. His mother cried, 'Should you not write to us as to how you are – and should you not visit your home at least on a Sunday?' Nagaraj on hearing it wanted to interject with, 'Why only Sunday? All days are Sundays in his case.' But he suppressed it and said, 'Exactly what I have also been trying to tell him . . .' Tim grunted a reply to his mother after a word of greeting and passed on to the bathroom. On the way he ran into his father coming out of the bath, who said, 'Don't run away. I have come to speak to you.'

Nagaraj felt relieved on hearing these words – which he felt, thankfully, were taken out of his mouth – and hoped Sita would leave him alone now and cease to behave like Lady Macbeth. It almost looked as if all his responsibilities were ended with the visit of his brother. He hoped he would take Tim away. Although his heart bled at the thought of his nephew's departure, he felt he needed respite from Sita's heckling and the strain of speculating about the young man.

He allotted the room in the second courtyard for his brother and his wife, feeling very nervous at first lest he should decline to go in there and insist upon sharing Tim's room. But this complication did not arise, the guests not minding where they were put up.

'Gopu, thank God,' thought Nagaraj, 'has grown rather mild in his talk and has refrained from calling his son "unleashed donkey".'

Gopu took the opportunity, when Tim was away in the

bathroom, to take Nagaraj aside and whisper to him, 'I have come with a purpose. A man from Delhi has come with the proposal for an alliance with our family, through Tim. The horoscopes are well matched . . . Are you listening?'

'Yes, yes,' said Nagaraj, feeling Gopu's good mood was getting exhausted and that he was reverting to his normal abrasiveness.

'You look sleepy – didn't you sleep last night?'

'Ah, yes. Gopu, now that you ask, I'm not able to sleep continuously nowadays, only broken sleep . . .'

'It's natural. You are not a youth to fall asleep like a log . . . but if you worked in the fields as I do, then it's different. You would sleep as if doped.'

'The king slept too soundly, and Macbeth finished him off in his sleep . . .' He suddenly thought of the line, 'Macbeth shall sleep no more . . .' but he had the self-control to say aloud, 'Sleep is important, of course, and what about the proposal from Delhi which you were mentioning?'

'Now listen, and don't put me to the trouble of repeating.'

Nagaraj sat up deferentially, and Gopu said, 'One Sriram from Delhi has sent his daughter's photo with her horoscope and has written to ask if we would consider a marriage proposal. I don't know how they came to know about us, particularly about our boy, who seems to be quite famous. Ha! Ha! If he had really done well in his studies, how nicely it would have fitted in. I don't want to go into all that now . . .'

'True, true,' echoed Nagaraj, feeling relieved that Gopu was not going into inconvenient details. Gopu turned round to ask, 'What do you mean by "true, true"? You keep saying "true, true" like a parrot, but do you know what the Truth is?'

'"What is Truth?" asked the Jesting Pilate and did not wait for an answer,' thought Nagaraj but shot off at a tangent, 'What about the horoscopes?'

'I told you they are perfectly matched,' answered Gopu.

'An astrologer said no two horoscopes suit each other so perfectly in his experience. They are offering ten thousand rupees dowry, and silver, etc. Excellent in every way, only I hope the fellow will prove worthy of it. The girl will come to Trichy in a couple of days and they want the boy to see her – '

'The girl must see the boy,' Nagaraj said in his desire to show an intelligent response.

'Goes without saying. How can the girl help not seeing when the boy stands before her in solid flesh? You say the most obvious things, unless you fear that the girl will shut her eyes at the sight of our fellow . . .'

Nagaraj felt obliged to laugh at the joke.

'What are you laughing at?' asked Gopu in irritation.

'Nothing, nothing, go on, tell me more,' said Nagaraj mollifyingly.

Gopu said, 'I have to take him to Trichy. Now tickets to be bought. I have a cousin in Trichy on Charu's side with whom we can stay for a day.'

Meanwhile the young man came out of the room dressed to go out. Gopu said, 'We have an important matter to tell you.'

'What is it?' asked the boy in a surly manner. Nagaraj, feeling that his presence might prove inhibiting, unobtrusively moved off to his seat on the pyol, leaving father and son alone to talk. Nagaraj was nervous lest an explosion of tempers might occur, but he was also trying to hear what they were saying to each other. Their voices receded and he guessed that they might have gone into Tim's room and shut the door. Nagaraj wondered what could be going on inside, whether they were going to emerge tearing each other apart in a deadly combat, in a state of what historians were fond of calling 'challenge and response'. To his surprise, both of them came out to the pyol verandah smiling, leaving Nagaraj to wonder what miracle had occurred. He had never in his experience seen Gopu beaming and Tim so cheerful. Tim told his father, 'Uncle must also come with us.'

'Why?' asked Gopu. 'Not necessary at this stage. Later . . .'

Tim said, 'He must also come,' persistently, as often as Gopu said, 'Not necessary'. But it was all in the style of pleasant exchange of views, a playful debate. Nagaraj wanted to know what it was all about but lacked the courage to question too much. He just sat smiling and looking pleasant lest his brother should accuse him of being sleepy, if silent, or too inquisitive if he questioned. Gopu came and sat on the pyol. Tim turned on his heels, picked up his bicycle and was off without saying a single word. Gopu looked after him and remarked, 'Where is he going so early in the day?'

A difficult question for Nagaraj. He gave a short laugh and murmured, 'Young men these days have so many things to do . . .' and before Gopu should turn around and say something about his studies, asked, 'Where does Tim want me to go?'

'Oh that!' said Gopu indulgently. 'To Trichy when we go there to see the girl.'

'Oh! Why me? What about Sita?'

'You should learn to survive without your wife sometimes. Of course, he wanted Sita also to be present, but I said no. We can't take a crowd at this stage. Later, when the marriage is settled, we may all go together in company . . . But he somehow insists on your coming. I had to agree because I don't want him to be a lost donkey. A marriage will tame him and tether him to a . . .'

'Tether him to what?' asked Nagaraj, unable to contain his curiosity.

'Of course, not to a lamppost, but to a domestic life – what a question!' replied Gopu.

'Has he agreed? How did you manage?'

'I'm not such an idiot as not to know that he is not going to college. I have sources of information; I know what is going on at this end. You keep things away from me but I know. I know all that goes on here. Do you know that he is working at a shady place called Kismet?'

'No, I don't.'

'He comes home late – and you don't even ask where he is going and what keeps him out so late every day!'

'He won't tell me anything,' confessed Nagaraj pathetically.

Gopu laughed at him. 'And you have no . . .' Nagaraj realised that Gopu was getting into his original form. He said admiringly, 'You should have been a detective. How much information you have managed to gather sitting in the village! Clever fellow!'

Gopu felt flattered and said, 'I am in touch with my old friends, who write to me or drop in when they happen to pass my way.' He added, 'I told him all that I knew about his activities but assured him that I don't mind what has happened if he will come on this trip to Trichy, and he at once agreed.'

Sita and her sister-in-law came out. Sita said, 'We want to see the morning puja at the temple for the good news that has come our way today.' They left. The engineer at the last house, starting out on his first visit to the bar, halted his steps for a minute to cry, 'Good morning, good brothers, good to see good brothers first thing in the good morning,' and passed on.

CHAPTER 10

'Marriages are made in heaven, but this is no heaven in any sense. Nor are angelic faces to be seen . . .' Nagaraj reflected, as he looked around the small hall in which they were seated on a Persian carpet, which seemed incongruous in these surroundings cluttered with odds and ends of old furniture pieces, and walls covered with scores of fading group photos or pock-marked with nails. Tim wore a blue shirt over his jeans and had tousled his hair to look like an off-stage film actor on the cover of the cinema magazines found on the table at Kismet lounge. His father, Gopu, had donned a silk shirt, wrapping a gaudy shawl around his shoulders, and had splashed his forehead with sandal paste and vermilion, acquiring thus a religious air which seemed to intimidate their hosts, consisting of the man from Delhi, his spouse, and some nondescript cousin hovering around.

Noisy untamed children were running round and round the verandah pillars. Nagaraj felt irritated. 'What would happen if I ordered, "Keep these dreadful children away! We are here to see a bride, not to watch these devils"? How different Tim was when he was a child, although his father sees in him now only an unleashed donkey. Poor boy, how anxiously he is waiting for his girl: rather a discouraging prospect since everyone in their group, men, women, and children, look some obscure foreign types with narrow eyes and high cheekbones, of a shade less than coffee.' Obviously out of the same mould of the man from Delhi. And all those awful children were his, displaying the same pattern in various grades, two-year-olds toddling about out to ten-year-olds, boys and girls all alike. Nagaraj felt curious to see their mother, perhaps she might be different, one hoped – and the girl might take after the mother. He noticed Gopu sitting like a yogi on the incongruous Persian carpet and looking imposing; if he could be photographed in colour they might make a calendar picture to hang on a wall.

Nagaraj abruptly asked the Delhi man, just to make conversation, 'Have you a photographer?'

The Delhi man, who was fidgeting about nervously, said, 'I had a photograph taken before leaving, but the copy will come by post. Anyway you will be seeing her now.'

Nagaraj did not correct him but said, 'Of course, no hurry.'

Gopu said pontifically, 'Why a photograph, when you can see the person directly? Photographs are, after all . . .'

Tim, who was reclining in an old easy chair, all tense and expectant, murmured, 'They say that the studios in Delhi are hopeless, always rushed and careless.'

The Delhi man did not want to contradict a prospective son-in-law and added, 'Life in Delhi is not what it used to be . . .'

At this point, Nagaraj wanted to question what this man's status was in Delhi, but restrained himself, afraid of Gopu's reaction, since he realised that this whole episode had developed from the magic phrase 'man from Delhi', proposing an alliance. Nagaraj wanted to ask, 'What are we waiting for? Where is the girl?' An incense stick wafting some exotic scent disturbed him. He felt disgusted. Meanwhile, he found Gopu enquiring of the gentlemen, 'Where did you get this carpet?' while Nagaraj would have asked, 'How did you manage to acquire this gorgeous carpet and why, since your cousin seems to live in this house which looks to be an enlarged cowshed?'

At the next stage, fruits and refreshments were served. Tim ate with relish everything placed before him, taking it as a foretaste of the father-in-law's hospitality for the rest of his life. Gopu tasted everything in elegant little doses as an act of graceful formality. Nagaraj had to follow his example though he felt like gorging himself. When it was finished and the dishes were carried away, a silver plate with betel leaves to chew was brought in by a lady and placed before them with a flourish. She was middle-aged and Nagaraj guessed she must be the mother of the bride-to-be, and felt relieved, after studying her face surreptitiously, that she was not foreign-looking; though plain, she had regular features, normal eyes and moderate cheekbones. She suddenly stooped low and whispered in her husband's ear, and he laughed artificially and said, 'Of course, if she is ready.' And he turned to the visitors and said, 'Saroja is ready, says my wife.'

Nagaraj asked inaudibly, 'Why do you say "my wife"? Is she her mother or not? And who is Saroja, why don't you say "daughter"?'

Presently, as if the curtains rose on a stage, led by her mother the bride-to-be appeared: a thick-set girl in a blue lace sari, bedecked with jewellery head to foot. She shyly entered, with eyes fixed on the ground. 'Oh, her eyes, hardly to be located between the eyebrows and high cheeks, how can we judge? Poor Tim will have no chance of judging her looks if she doesn't lift her chin. How will she know what Tim looks like? Is this how marriages are mismanaged in heaven? She is definitely alien-looking, and I pray Tim will refuse.' Nagaraj watched Tim to know if he would avert his eyes, but found him gazing at her in open-mouthed wonder.

Gopu was staring at her unabashedly to evaluate her personality. Nagaraj commented to himself, 'Whatever she may be, the ten-thousand dowry is the real attraction for Gopu. He doesn't seem to care how Tim is going to spend the rest of his life with a companion possessing the sort of face I used to see in geographical magazines at the Town Hall reading room.' Coming back to the earth he noticed the girl throwing a lingering glance at Tim who, open-eyed, was drinking in her personality. 'Poor fellow! Never knew he'd be so weak-minded. Must warn him not to say "yes" to this proposal. How to tolerate the girl's presence day in and day out if Tim decides to continue to live in Kabir Street with his wife?'

The girl's father induced her to sit down with a harmonium and sing. She protested coyly at first, but yielded. Her voice was nasal. Nagaraj didn't like the cheap coarse lilt of the tune. He shut his eyes, unable to stand the spectacle of the girl opening and closing her lips, exposing her teeth while singing.

Her father said, 'She is singing a famous song from the latest Hindi film. She has learnt it by herself. Once she hears a tune, that is enough; she doesn't have to be taught, she can repeat it. She knows over a hundred songs, all self-taught. Gramophone companies want her to record but I say, "Not yet." She must complete her M.A. first.' He seemed extremely proud of his daughter. He added, 'In Delhi young people have opportunities to develop their talents. She is a member of a group, often called to perform at social functions, colleges, schools, and clubs.'

Gopu and Tim were properly impressed. Gopu uttered many sounds of appreciation while Saroja sang, nodding his head appropriately. Nagaraj also imitated him to some extent out of politeness but, as usual, his head was buzzing with other ideas. 'I am no expert in music, but I can distinguish between melody and nasal whining. Poor Tim, I hope he will not be carried away.'

But actually Tim was not only impressed but overwhelmed. As he told his uncle later, 'In Delhi girls are smart.' Nagaraj felt despondent, but restrained himself, just emitting some affirmative noises. Gopu kept talking about the Delhi family and made several complimentary remarks about it. Nagaraj asked, 'When will you get the dowry in hand?'

'Right away, as soon as we give the approval – they'll be coming here tomorrow.'

'Have you spoken to Tim?'

'Not necessary. He said he would come by the next bus.'

Nagaraj understood that from the sales point of view he must have encouraged Tim to stay back.

Two days later Tim was back in Kabir Street and was full of praise for the Delhi family. Nagaraj felt it would be impolitic and futile to express his views or ask formally if Tim liked the girl.

CHAPTER II

Nagaraj found it irksome, being used to the silence of his home, where even street noises were muffled by the heavy door and the occasional monologues uttered by Sita in the kitchen fell in tune with the surroundings. Now he found his peace disturbed.

Tim and his wife Saroja occupied the middle room, just as Gopu and his wife had done in the past, with this difference: when the Gopus shut themselves in, one never heard any sound outside, but now one's ears were assailed with the incessant chatter and giggling emanating from the room until Tim left for Kismet (or wherever it might be) at his usual hour. Saroja then started reading aloud from a cinema magazine, followed by a sudden burst of singing to the accompaniment of her harmonium. It was this part of her programme that distracted Nagaraj most. Although the door was shut, her harmonium seemed to pierce the walls and the doors. Nagaraj would say to himself, 'Ganesha be thanked that she is not learning the violin, otherwise . . .' It was his nature to feel grateful for small mercies. He tried to face the trial by staying away on the pyol, shutting the main door firmly behind him. But still the music pursued him and he could not watch the street life with abandon.

He wondered if he had an aversion to music itself. 'No,' he reflected, 'I was the founder of the Saraswati Sabha at one time and collected funds for classical concerts held at the primary school hall in Vinayak Street, but had to abandon it eventually for lack of support. But I listen to music now and then and enjoy it. I cannot pursue it as a full-time job like my friend Natesh, who started a rival music association years ago, and still runs it. But he is a music teacher, has contacts at Madras and makes money out of the concerts. It is a full-time job but not for me – one who has so much to do and think constantly on, ah, Narada himself, who was the guardian of music. His music never ceased, heard or unheard.'

Nagaraj suddenly remembered Keats' lines, 'Heard melodies are sweet, but those unheard are sweeter'. Why should he not go up and knock on Saroja's door, and ask if the girl knew Keats and would she make her melody unheard? He suddenly felt like praying to Narada himself, though a part of his mind kept echoing: no one ever prayed to one who was only a celestial wanderer and sage. 'Oh, great divine sage,' he inaudibly appealed, 'please give that girl better sense than to sing, and inspire her not to deafen us with her harmonium and film hits.' As if in response to his prayer, the sound of music ceased, and Nagaraj at once said to himself, 'Narada! You are a god, I now understand. Forgive my doubts. Give me the power to write about you; when it comes out, men and women will worship you. But how am I to proceed? I must find a pundit who knows the subject.'

The pause in music was welcome – but could be temporary. Saroja is perhaps looking through her notebook for more songs or perhaps (this was a more embarrassing prospect) she must be coming out to ask sweetly, 'Uncle, how did you like my singing?' It had happened before and he was torn between candour and diplomacy. He did not want to face a similar predicament now. His mind was made up. He briskly got up, went in, dressed, and left the house after a brief explanation to Sita.

Kavu pundit, who lived in 64, IV Cross, Ellaman Lane, off Ellaman Street, had been recommended to him by the old librarian at the Town Hall. Nagaraj was now undertaking a trip to Ellaman Street, which he had often crossed once upon a time during his evening stroll in Coomar's company. Kavu pundit lived in an ancient tiled shed with two coconut trees framing its entrance over a gutter. The pundit was lying in an easy chair with his feet on its arms and was staring ahead at nothing in particular. Nagaraj announced himself, 'Town Hall librarian has asked me to see you.'

'He is my mother's sister's son. Long time since we met. Did he tell you we are cousins?'

Nagaraj nodded noncommittally and mentioned his purpose. The old man became alert and sat up, lowering his feet from the chair arm. 'Do you know Sanskrit grammar?' he asked suddenly.

Nagaraj shook his head and would have added, 'Why Sanskrit grammar, I am ignorant of any grammar. When I was in Albert Mission, I was . . .'

'You are suddenly lost in thought?' asked the pundit. 'Is it very important?'

'Yes, yes,' said Nagaraj, squirming in his seat – a wooden chair, loose jointed, which rocked precariously when he was seized with a fit of sneezing whenever the pundit inhaled a pinch of snuff. It shook and creaked all through their conversation. He could not complete his sentence, being preoccupied with maintaining his balance in his chair. He had wanted to confess, 'I was thrown out of the classroom once for not explaining the difference between an adjective and an adverb and also between a noun and a pronoun.' But as usual he was discreet enough to remain silent. 'You are quiet,' commented the scholar with a slight smile, which produced on his face a regular web of wrinkles, unsuspected normally as he seemed smooth-cheeked when he did not smile. Nagaraj suppressed his thoughts and said, 'I have not had the good fortune to learn Sanskrit – only English and Tamil.'

The pundit said, 'I am not surprised. Sanskrit is not a bazaar language. it is known as "Deva Basha". Do you know what it means?'

'"Language of Gods",' translated Nagaraj promptly, feeling proud of his answer and almost looking as if he expected to be rewarded with an almond peppermint, as was the custom in those days when his father helped him through homework.

'At least you know this much; I am glad. Are you aware Sanskrit cannot be picked up at any wayside shop? You must have performed meritorious deeds in several births to be blessed with a tongue that could spell the Sanskrit alphabet.'

'Ah, what wisdom, perhaps one's ears too must be blessed to hear the Sanskrit sound,' added Nagaraj, much to the delight of the pundit. More wrinkles appeared on his face as his smile broadened. Nagaraj added to the pleasure of this dialogue by saying, 'God creates a scholar like your good self to kindle the flame of knowledge in an ignoramus like me.'

'Ah, do not degrade yourself,' said the pundit. 'You talk like a poet, no wonder you want to engage yourself in kavya.' Nagaraj knew enough Sanskrit not to ask, 'What is kavya?'

The pundit cross-examined, 'Do you know how the phrase has been formed?'

Nagaraj felt he might step into a trap any minute and diverted the talk into other channels. 'In our schools, Sanskrit is neglected.'

'Do you know why?'

Nagaraj hesitated to answer, wondering if it would prove a trap again. He wanted to blurt out what he had often heard: that Sanskrit was a dead language and no one cared, but he feared it might upset the pundit and so he said, 'Because there are no proper teachers.'

The pundit let out a shout of approval and added, 'Too true! How can any pundit teach with walls around in a classroom? Do you know how many scnools have approached me?'

'Must be hundreds,' Nagaraj said, to be on the safe side.

'Not so many, but twenty-five schools and colleges. We

do not have more than twenty-five even if we counted the colleges outside . . .'

Nagaraj felt he need not listen too intently to his talk, which seemed to stray farther and farther from the purpose of his visit, and he switched off his mind while appearing to be listening. The other added, 'For Sanskrit studies our schools are unsuited; they are all right for English and other mlecha bashas . . .' Again, Nagaraj knew enough Sanskrit to understand what was mlecha basha ('outcast's language') and he felt an urge to dispute this definition since he loved the English language, though his application to its studies was vague and haphazard and he had obtained only marginal credit for his performance in the examinations.

Meanwhile, the pundit was elaborating. 'Do you know how we used to learn or where we were taught? Always on the steps of the river. When it rained we assembled in a temple hall, sitting beside the stone pillar without leaning back. We had to sit erect when our teacher recited, and we had to repeat after him. We needed no books or pencils – everything had to go through only the ear and stay there.' And he tapped his forehead. 'We recited with our master, even while bathing or washing clothes. We were learning at all hours, our masters never leaving our side – no other occupation for at least twelve years or more until our masters were satisfied.'

'What is your impression of Narada?' Nagaraj asked, realising that it was time to remind the pundit of the purpose of his visit.

'Who am I to pass a judgement on a great soul?'

Nagaraj realised his phrasing was wrong. 'In your studies you must have – '

The other cut him short with, 'You want to listen to his life story?'

'Yes, that is my ambition, my life's aim, you may call it.'

The pundit said, 'Even if you lived through ten births, you would not reach the end of his life story.'

'What should I do now?' Nagaraj asked, puzzled by his answer.

'Go and sit on the river step and meditate and the answer will come. But you will get nowhere near your theme by wearing a silk shirt with a gold fountain pen peeping out of your pocket. You must observe austerity.'

Nagaraj wanted to protest, 'What I am wearing is not silk but cotton and my pen is not gold but Watermans, my father's, costing ten rupees in those days. If my brother had noticed it he would have claimed it as his share of the property,' but as usual he swallowed his words and remained silent.

'Ah, you are scared of meditation. Why?'

'I have not been taught it but I have ochre robes in my puja room.'

'Who gave you ochre clothes?'

'My guru.'

'Who is he? There are so many charlatans around us.'

'I know him only as Swamiji. I have lost sight of him. He probably vanished into the Himalayas.'

The pundit laughed and said, 'Unwise, unwise to believe such nonsense.'

Nagaraj felt confused and annoyed at the turn their talk was taking. He was wondering if he could get up without any ceremony and run away, when the other suddenly got up from his seat, went in, and came back carrying four heavy red volumes in his arms, and placed them on a low stool. 'If you read these, you will understand Narada. You may come here and study them every day.'

'May I look through the pages?'

'Yes.'

Nagaraj timidly picked up a volume and turned the leaves. 'All in Sanskrit!' he cried.

'What did you expect? Bazaar language?'

'I have confessed, I do not know Sanskrit.'

'Of course you did. What if? This is just to indicate that you are a nothing without Sanskrit; it must be a lesson to you.'

'If you will kindly read and explain,' began Nagaraj.

'You think I have nothing better to do?'

'I can pay any fee.'

The master looked outraged. 'Do you take me to be a peddler of knowledge? If you are blind and deaf to Sanskrit, who gave you the idea you should attempt the "Great Sage"?'

'In a dream some voice ordered that I should attempt the subject.'

'Then go back to that dream; do not come here,' said the pundit, picked up his volumes and turned in.

Nagaraj felt desolate and stood transfixed, staring after the retreating scholar, hoping that he might relent and come back. He reappeared on the step only to wave Nagaraj off finally, saying, 'Go and write the fable of the inquisitive monkey who had his balls crushed when he sat on a split log and pulled out the wedge, in any basha you please, but leave grand subjects alone.'

Nagaraj retraced his steps, went down the lane, sunk in thought. He turned towards the river, ploughing his way through the sands, still warm with the day's sun. Evening time, habitual loungers at the riverside here and there, a sight which revived his spirits.

He had felt rather shocked at the turn the pundit's mood and words had taken. Such a fanatic for Sanskrit. 'The world is ruined by such fanatics. After all, language has a purpose, which could be served without so much madness. What did the pundit take himself to be – a world teacher, while he seemed no better than the humble priest who came home and recited Sanskrit mantras on ceremonial occasions for a fee of twenty-five paise? Kavu pundit was only a swollen-headed version of that class and perhaps must have performed funeral rites for two rupees in his days, though he professes to be a unique scholar now! He and his four red volumes! Those pages probably contained trash, who could say? Even our priest must be keeping such imposing volumes in his house – must be a part of the show, a standard equipment.' He felt a peculiar satisfaction at the memory of their visiting priest being heckled for unpunctuality in those days when rituals were performed regularly at home. Even that priest must have spent twelve years memorising lessons on the river steps.

Ah, the river steps. He recollected the advice to meditate on the river steps. Why not try? The only sane thing the pundit had uttered was to direct him there to meditate. Wondering how one meditated, he walked on to the river steps, ten granite steps leading down to the water's edge with water flowing along softly.

He went down and sat on the last step with his feet touching the cold water. He felt suddenly a glow of satisfaction at having taken a step forward towards Narada. Age-old banyan trees canopying the river's edge rustled, and birds settling on the branches cackled and chirped. 'Would be difficult to meditate in this uproar,' he thought. He contemplated the flowing river and all his doubts vanished. If he had a sheet of paper, he would have spread it and begun the first line. What would be the first line, he asked himself. 'Narada was a great sage . . .' No doubt it would be some beginning, better than no beginning. Critics might say, 'Ah, what a discovery!' and heap insults on the author for being banal. Difficult profession. Why should I bother to write and produce a book when my father has left me a house and enough to live on comfortably? Why did any author produce a book? Because he wanted cash. But I do not care for it – even at Boeing Centre I do free work, declining the money offered; rightly too. Did not some philosopher declare: all money is evil? Somehow I am not attracted to it. Otherwise one would have developed like Coomar, who was once such a simple soul, now earning thousands an hour, but watchful night and day to make more and more money and avoid tax. He has also become showy, wears a lace turban and a buttoned-up silk coat over a lace dhoti, and has moved from his ancient home at Ellaman Street to New Extension. Feels too great to be seen in his old surroundings, never walks, always riding in a motorcar with a driver to open the door and all that. No time to chat with anyone. Only weavers from the villages, his companions all day at the Centre. Probably drinks at night, resuming his old habit.

Nagaraj checked his thoughts, realising that Coomar could not have been the subject of meditation suggested by the haughty pundit. He had said meditate on the river steps, and not meditate on Coomar, who had his faults, but was still a good friend, a great friend. Meditate? How to meditate? On what?

Nagaraj realised when he tried meditation, whatever it meant, his thoughts wandered in all directions and were in a jumble. Perhaps he should press his fingers to his nostrils; stop breathing and close his eyes. He attempted this course for one second and felt suffocated. His eyes darkened, and he was on the point of abandoning it all when he felt a pat on his back and nearly tumbled into the river. He feared that Narada had responded and was manifesting himself. He turned around and saw his neighbour, the Talkative Man, standing over him with a grin.

'Oh, T.M., you! Least expected here. What are you up to?'

The Talkative Man came down and sat by his side, dipping his feet in the running water.

'I had to meet a man in Ellaman Street and thought I could as well visit the river. What brings you here?'

'Oh, this is my favourite retreat, I come here often.'

'Formerly with your inseparable friend Coomar,' added the Talkative Man.

Nagaraj said, 'You notice everything.'

'I can't be a journalist otherwise. I must be everywhere and see a lot – even if my paper publishes only three lines of my report.'

'Can you tell me about Narada?' asked Nagaraj suddenly.

'Which Narada? Who is he?' asked the Talkative Man.

To the tune of the rustling banyan leaves overhead, Nagaraj explained his preoccupation and asked, 'Can you take me to someone who will help me?'

The Talkative Man thought over it and said, 'Why on earth do you want to write about Narada?'

Having once been inspired to mention a dream, Nagaraj felt that it saved much explanation, and said, 'I was commanded in a dream.'

The Talkative Man laughed and said, 'You are becoming quite a mystic really. Next you will be miracle healing with a pinch of sacred ash.'

Nagaraj did not know whether to accept it as a compliment or a joke. The Talkative Man would not let him rest there. He prodded him further and enjoyed it. 'Why not?' he asked. 'After all, most of your time you spend on the pyol. Why not gather your devotees there?'

Nagaraj accepted the honour with due modesty although troubled by a doubt that the other might not be serious. 'That will be as God wills it. If I can be of service to our fellow beings, I will not hesitate, though not at present. Later, perhaps when my writing is over . . . Now I have to write about the sage and you must help me find a teacher.'

'Why don't you ask the one who commanded you in your dream? He must be the right person.'

Nagaraj did not appreciate the Talkative Man's frivolous attitude, and regretted mentioning his mission which should have lain as a secret to be imparted only to worthy ears. The pundit's attitude was unhelpful. He began to doubt if he would ever get any help or would have to abandon the subject altogether. He threw his mind back and tried to find out why he had chosen Narada. He said to himself, 'It is probably a divine will.'

The other watched his face and asked, 'Can't you get back to the dream?'

Nagaraj replied, 'I wish I could, but for the moment I need a pundit's help to do research. I ask you, but you also talk like Kavu pundit, who asked me to go back to the dream!' He laughed bitterly at the memory of it.

The Talkative Man pricked up his ears. 'Did you say Kavu pundit? The very person I was about to suggest.'

'He would not help me,' confessed Nagaraj in a sad tone.

'Why not?'

'Because I did not know Sanskrit.'

'Very reasonable objection. He is a firebrand where Sanskrit is concerned. But he is the only man in our town who can help you.'

'But he has rejected me already.'

'When did you see him?'

'About an hour ago.'

'He will have cooled off now. Come with me. I'll talk to him.'

Nagaraj regretted mentioning the pundit. Never expected he would be forced to go back to him. He felt uneasy at the prospect of meeting him again, but the Talkative Man was insistent.

'Come with me, he won't say no to me. You should have told me first.'

'But it is impossible to stop and talk to you when you leave home in the morning, although I see you every day.'

'Never mind all that. Come with me now.' Nagaraj felt panicky.

'Oh no, not now . . .'

The Talkative Man seized his arm and almost pulled him up. Nagaraj wondered what this man's secret was that he should feel so confident of his power over the odious pundit. The Talkative Man said, 'He lives close by.'

'I know it,' Nagaraj cried. 'I have no doubt he will throw me out again.'

'He won't. Come with me, you will see the difference.'

'If he sees my face again, I do not know what he will do.'

'I will be there. Don't fear.' Nagaraj felt helpless as the other piloted him across the stretch of sand and back to 64, Ellaman Lane.

He stayed back beside the two coconut trees over the dry gutter at the entrance. The Talkative Man went up and knocked on the door. The pundit appeared and greeted him with apparent pleasure. 'Oh Ramu!' he cried. 'Where have you been all these months? So rare nowadays!'

'I have to move around all day: visiting courts, police stations and various meetings, etc. Nearly twenty miles a day and then to the railway station to post my report.'

'Do you earn enough for all your trouble, or do they cheat you?' the old man asked, leading him to the wooden chair and lowering himself on the easy chair. 'Back on his throne,' commented Nagaraj, watching from behind the coconut trees. 'What is the secret of the Talkative Man's hold on him? He calls him Ramu, never thought he was Ramu.' The old man was saying, 'You must marry. How long are you going to remain a lone vagrant?'

'Uncle, no one will marry me,' said the Talkative Man in mock sorrow. The conversation was proceeding on these lines when the pundit all of a sudden noticed the figure of Nagaraj beside the coconut trees. He shaded his eyes with his palm and asked, 'I see someone there, who is it?'

The Talkative Man said, 'He is my friend, came with me and is waiting.'

'Oh, your friend! Why do you keep him off? Let him come in.'

Nagaraj never suspected that the pundit could assume such an affable tone and wondered again what secret hold the Talkative Man had on him. The Talkative Man hailed, 'Nagaraj, come here! Pundit wants you.'

Nagaraj hesitated, thinking, 'I am not the pundit's slave to be summoned or thrown out as he pleases.' He tried to shrink out of sight and took a few steps back. At this the Talkative Man dashed forward and caught hold of Nagaraj before he could escape. 'Why is this fellow taking so much interest in me? I had better abandon my project.' The Talkative Man tightened his hold on his shoulder till he cried, 'It hurts, leave me . . .' The other would not be deflected from his purpose. 'What an awful fellow! Delights in tormenting me. I wish I had not set eyes on him today,' reflected Nagaraj.

The Talkative Man propelled him before the pundit. He looked him over and cried, 'This fellow, I have seen him somewhere.'

'Sit down, sit down.' The Talkative Man pushed Nagaraj down on the wooden chair and squatted cross-legged on the floor.

'I have seen him somewhere,' the pundit kept repeating.

The Talkative Man said, 'So many visit you to seek your guidance, but you cannot be expected to remember every face. He is my particular friend and neighbour. Very rich, but he has only academic interests unlike other rich men, who only want to squander their cash.'

'Ah!' cried the old man, turning to Nagaraj. 'Very rare indeed. What's your interest?'

The Talkative Man promptly answered, 'He wants to learn all about the great seer Narada.'

'Narada! Is this the same fellow who came earlier?'

The Talkative Man said casually, 'So many are interested in that sage nowadays, quite a popular subject. Last week alone I heard the subject mentioned by at least seven persons, and I will send a news report if I find some more people having an interest in the subject. It's a new phenomenon.'

'Is that so? Wait a minute,' said the pundit, getting up. He went in and emerged with the four red volumes in his arms, dumped them on the stool and said, 'In here you will find everything about the great saint's birth, growth and achievements.'

'You are the right guru for my friend here. Help him.'

'I suspect he is the same fellow.'

'What if!' cried the Talkative Man. 'This world has many men looking alike and wanting to write on Narada.'

The old man repeated, 'I suspect it is the same fellow.'

'Do not call him "fellow". He belongs to one of the oldest Kabir Street families, aristocrats all of them.'

'All grand families,' agreed the pundit. 'I was once related to one of those families through my wife's uncle. She is no more. I am all alone in this house, depending on a servant for my survival.'

The Talkative Man made sounds of sympathy. Nagaraj remained moody and silent, not being sure what would be a proper remark.

The old man said, 'Take a look at those books and see what you can get out of those pages. But you must come and read here. I won't let the volumes out of sight.'

Nagaraj felt desperate, but felt obliged to pick up a volume and pretend to scan the imposing lines on a page. He was wondering how to extricate himself from the situation when the old man suggested, 'Read it aloud, you will then realise how beautiful the composition is. It is one of those classics composed partly in prose and partly in poetry. Such a composition is known as . . .' He mentioned some technical term.

Nagaraj by now had reached a state of desperation and announced, 'I cannot read this.'

'Why?' asked the pundit.

The Talkative Man came to his rescue. He said, 'Uncle, you have heard of Dr Sripathy?'

'No,' said the old man. 'I know no doctor. I am not like you, wandering about meeting people.'

Added the Talkative Man, 'No one expects it at your age. But let me tell you that Sripathy is a famous eye surgeon, and he had ordered my friend not to read for some time to come. He is not to strain his eyes.'

'How is he going to write?'

'He can listen to your reading, no time limit to it, and then dictate as he pleases. So I suggest you read out and explain, and he will dedicate the book to you and acknowledge your help, in bold print, and when it is ready I'll make it world news and people will come crowding from Europe and America not only to see the author but more than that his guru responsible for the masterpiece.'

The pundit was pleased to hear it, and the Talkative Man made the scheme acceptable further when he suggested a fee for the tuition: one hundred and fifty rupees to be paid on the first of every month as long as the lessons lasted. The old man was beside himself with joy. He said, however, 'Money is unimportant. If this fellow listens and understands, it is more than enough, but if he is a dunce and expects me to repeat things, I do not want him.'

'He is very intelligent,' announced the Talkative Man. 'Otherwise I would not bring him before you. Can you expect less from a Kabir Street family?'

'You are right, Ramu. If you had told me at the start his family background, I would not have asked any question.'

The Talkative Man finalised the arrangement. Turning to Nagaraj he asked, 'Do you start tomorrow?'

Before he could answer, the pundit interposed to say, 'Let me look into the almanac and find an auspicious day and hour for starting the lessons.'

'When will you see the almanac?' asked the Talkative Man.

'Tomorrow morning after my puja. I won't touch it now.'

'Then tomorrow morning?' and the Talkative Man nudged Nagaraj and whispered, 'Take out your purse and give him an advance.'

The pundit received the advance thankfully and asked, 'What do you call your friend?'

'Nagaraj . . . we call him Nag.'

'Don't. Nagaraj is a holy name, don't spoil it. Nagaraj means King of Serpents, which means "Adi Sesha", the thousand-hooded serpent in whose coils God's Vishnu rests, though some ignorant upstarts want to maintain that "Nagaraj" means not "Adi Sesha" but "Vasuki".' He laughed at the absurdity of it. The Talkative Man and Nagaraj joined in, the Talkative Man remarking, 'People will go to any length to pervert things.'

They were supposed to start their lessons at an auspicious hour and the day was to be fixed by the pundit. Meanwhile, Nagaraj had to go up daily to see the pundit to know when.

His daily routine underwent a change. He had to cut short his stay at the Silk Centre and leave at two-thirty instead of four after rushing through his ledger work. On the way he stopped at the Boardless for coffee. Varma, the proprietor of the Boardless, became curious. 'You were one of those late evening men. Why are you so early?'

Nagaraj felt important while explaining, 'I am going through some Sanskrit studies.'

Varma had no interest in it but uttered a general agreement, 'Very important. If I had the time, I would have joined you. But if I leave this desk, who will take care of things here? One has to watch unwinkingly, otherwise business will suffer, reputation for quality will go. One has to watch unwinkingly . . .'

Nagaraj reflected, 'Like a dozen others in the trade, he begins a monologue on money matters.' He paid for the coffee and left. It was tedious to walk the couple of miles every day, but there was no transport system, except for a handful of autorickshaws, but they congregated at the market gate and no driver would agree to drive in the direction of Ellaman Lane even if a return trip was guaranteed.

'It is good exercise,' he said to himself. 'Walking also stimulates the brain,' he had read in a magazine. 'Narada moved through the universe on foot. Did he wait for an autorickshaw? Even if there were autorickshaws available for a celestial ride, the driver would probably have said, "I can't come in that direction. No return fare from that loka. No one is known to return from that loka (if it happened to be Yama's – the god of death)."'

Nagaraj laughed to himself at this fantasy. 'Must lighten my text with such humour. Readers will appreciate it. Otherwise it will be a heavy tome. Anyway, let me hope that I will make a start. I do not know what the pundit has in mind. He has starting trouble like Coomar's motorcar, which has to be pushed every day a good distance before the driver could take the wheel.' The pundit's starting trouble seemed to be the auspicious moment, which seemed to be elusive.

The moment Nagaraj appeared before him, the pundit showed him his seat on the rickety chair and took a pinch of snuff which blew in the air and brought Nagaraj to the point of sneezing and falling off the chair. The pundit always asked, 'Why do you sneeze so much? You must see your doctor . . .' Nagaraj dared not say it was the snuff; in a voice thick with sneezing, he would mumble a reply.

The pundit spent his time airing his views on the state of affairs in general. Nagaraj listened respectfully, hoping that at the end of a particular sentence he would rise, go inside the house and return with the red volumes. But no sign of it happening.

The pundit covered various antiquated subjects. He had no idea what the town looked like beyond Ellaman Street. He spent the time asking for an account of the state of the forest beyond the market. 'We lived in Vinayak Street, which was fairly safe, but never ventured in the evenings beyond the market; on the western side of it the forest began, and we admired the courage of the Kabir Street men who lived so close to the forest, where at dusk one heard the jackals howl and also the roar of a tiger, and quite often cattle in the sheds were carried away . . .' He went on and on in the same strain, ignoring the purpose of Nagaraj's visit. Nagaraj explained how it was now a different town and how New Extension had come up not only on the market boundary but also other developments beyond the railway level crossing.

'Do trains actually pass there?' the old man asked, and added, 'Some day I must go and look at the place. From your account it must be like London.'

Nagaraj could not help asking, 'Have you seen London?'

'Yes, of course, in pictures. My cousin is the librarian at the Town Hall. He used to bring me illustrated magazines. We were so close at one time. Nowadays, alas, I think he does not remember me.'

'Oh, no, he remembers, but he has retired and hardly goes out. The Talkative Man sees him some days, but he feels very old now . . .'

'What if? Who is not old or getting old? Is it something special to him? Tell him that he is a fool, that cousin of mine. Do you know that he is my grandmother's sister's son?'

'Yes, yes,' agreed Nagaraj, although he remembered hearing of some other relationship on the first day.

'You must keep in mind the truth of the proverb . . .' began the pundit.

'Which proverb?' Nagaraj could not help asking.

'Which proverb? I have forgotten. Yes, yes, it comes back to me. My grandmother used to utter it, that is, that librarian's grandmother-in-law's sister . . .'

'Now a new kinship?' Nagaraj thought, but resigned himself to accepting whatever relationship the old man hit upon at a time. 'What is the proverb, may I ask?'

'It says kinship vanishes uncherished and loan vanishes unasked.'

Nagaraj was impressed although he saw no connection between the two ideas. He kept wondering when the pundit would begin the lessons, but hinted, 'Narada, sir.'

'You fear that I have forgotten? Wrong, if you think so. Do not misjudge me.'

'Oh, no, don't mistake me, sir – '

'Because you have given me a hundred rupees, don't ever imagine that I am your slave to do your bidding.'

'Oh, no. I would not dream of such a thing. Since I did not notice the red volume, I was thinking it must be lost . . .' He went on rambling, unable to conclude the sentence, fearing anything he might say might go against him and the old man might order him to leave.

But he only said, 'Remember this. You are ignorant and young. How old are you?'

'Not too young,' Nagaraj had the recklessness to say and, inwardly, 'What is that to you?'

The old man said, 'What is the use of your coming at this hour when the sun is going? How can I read in this light?' Nagaraj had not the courage to correct him and assert that he had arrived before four.

'Should I come in the morning, sir?' he asked with humility.

'No, my pujas are important in the morning. I don't eat until the pujas are performed and all the gods are worshipped. Come in and see my puja room and look at the number of images I have to decorate with flowers and anoint with milk and honey.'

Thus ended one day's lessons. Nagaraj did not give up hope. He decided to readjust the hour of his visit. Next morning he went up to the first house on Kabir Street and knocked on the door. The Talkative Man opened it. Nagaraj explained his predicament. The Talkative Man said, 'You will have to persist. Go again and again until he starts. Once he starts, it will be difficult to stop him. Do you play cards?' he asked suddenly.

Nagaraj said, 'No, why?'

'He loves cards and card players. If you knew cards, he would not leave you but follow you about . . .'

'Alas, I do not know. How long will it take to learn?'

'You will have to be born with it.'

Nagaraj looked despondent. The Talkative Man said, 'You may as well come in and talk.'

Nagaraj tried to excuse himself but the Talkative Man brushed aside his objection. 'After all, your usual seat in the pyol won't go away.'

Nagaraj's nature had no resistance of any kind in it. The Talkative Man seated him in his drawing room and brought him a cup of coffee. 'Ah, you look surprised,' said the Talkative Man. 'I am quite well provided in the kitchen, able to make a few things for myself when needed. Otherwise I go to Varma who is my benefactor at most times. Now I have a little time today. The municipal meeting is postponed. About the pundit. He is a great scholar, but rather difficult. You must know how to handle him. Anyway, why don't you choose some other subject available if you are itching to write?'

'No, Narada is very important to present-day men and

women. He is a celestial sage who moved with ease among the gods.'

'A sage full of mischief and intrigue like a journalist,' said the Talkative Man, at which Nagaraj felt slightly upset. 'Wait till you see my book,' he said.

'Provided Kavu pundit makes up his mind,' sneered the Talkative Man, and added, 'If you knew cards you could have ordered him about.'

'Alas, I never learnt card playing.'

'Neither Sanskrit nor the cards. How do you expect to be accepted by the pundit? Why don't you start off with, "Narada was the author of card playing," and ask the pundit for confirmation?'

'I do not understand.'

'I must tell you Kavu pundit has spent a whole lifetime playing cards. I was young when his family lived in Vinayaka Street and I used to hang around playing with his sons and we always noticed him with three others, seated on the pyol of his house, holding cards in their hands and lost in a samadhi. He did no work except go out and give readings from sacred texts or the Ramayana at a temple in a nearby village four evenings in a week. He was popular and respected by his public; they used to send bullock carts to fetch him. While his evenings were spent in holy readings, his days were spent at cards. His wife, who is no more, suffered because he spent all his time in gambling, but she somehow managed. But after her death he was in a terrible mess. He borrowed from moneylenders, played for high stakes and continuously lost. Came a time when his creditors seized his house and he had to move out. He had a little cash and took on lease the shed in which he lives now in Ellaman Lane. If you wrote his life rather than Narada's you could write a best-seller and share the proceeds with him. The key to his heart lies in a game called "Twenty-Eight". I do not know much about it but you just ask him to teach you and he will be only too happy. In between, you could ask questions about Narada.'

Nagaraj could not decide, as usual, whether the Talkative Man was serious or joking, but pleaded, 'Please help me.'

'You will help yourself best only if you learn "Twenty-Eight" or abandon Narada.'

'Impossible,' said Nagaraj, taking it literally. 'The only difference I know in cards is that some are black and some red. Narada cannot be abandoned. It is my whole life's aim.'

'Well, I was only joking. It is a pity you have no use for cards. But I must confess I myself do not know much except what I picked up sitting behind friends at Kismet when I went there.'

'Do you see Tim at Kismet?'

'Of course, where else can I see him?'

'What does he do there? He is married,' reflected Nagaraj aloud.

'Well, what if? There is talk of his bringing his wife to sing. She will get paid for it.'

Nagaraj felt stunned. He never thought it would come to this. A daughter-in-law of the family to sing to a set of drunkards at Kismet. What would his brother say? His head was in a whirl. For the time being Kavu Pundit and Narada receded into the background. 'Saroja to carry her harmonium to New Extension . . . Will she carry it under her arm?' He remained in thought for a moment and asked suddenly, 'How will she take it there?'

'Maybe Tim will carry it for her.'

'They will look like street singers whom I have seen in a film long ago.'

'That was a good film in which Saigal or someone appeared. How do you remember it, wonderful!'

Nagaraj was in no mood to enjoy the compliment. He was worried what Sita would say or the neighbours or his brother, ever ready to pounce on him. 'You look terrified,' commented the Talkative Man, studying his face and enjoying his predicament. 'Don't worry. Let them do what they like. Young people of these days are different.'

'Can you do something about it? Talk to the manager and explain . . .'

'They see nothing wrong in it.'

Nagaraj rose, unable to contain his agitation. He merely said, 'I will not see the pundit today – another day.'

'Excellent idea. Leave him alone for some time, he must have food for thought. I will talk to him and then you can meet him. Meanwhile, see if you can invent stories around Narada. It will be nice if you can invent a series of short stories of Narada independently of Kavu pundit's lessons. Start with the story on hand: I am Narada bringing you a gossip item, which may develop into a family incident.'

Acting on the Talkative Man's advice, Nagaraj allowed three days to pass before meeting the pundit again. He timed his arrival early so that the pundit might not complain of a lack of sunlight during their session. The moment he appeared, the old gentleman cried, 'So early today. Why do you disturb me at this hour? I generally sleep for some time; if I don't, I feel giddy.' Nagaraj remained silent, not wishing to offer any explanation.

'Sit down, sit down.' Nagaraj sat in his usual chair, holding his breath while the old man took a punch of snuff and inhaled. The old man said, 'Why are you afraid of snuff? It is unmanly. Snuff keeps one alert. But for this, I wouldn't be able to talk to you. Do you know, in ancient texts snuff is mentioned not as tobacco powder but as ambrosia dust, inhaled before a warrior sets out to fight. Even the gods did it. Karthikeya, before setting out to destroy the asura, took several inhalations. In the Mahabaratha, in certain versions, it is mentioned that a truce was declared between the armies so as to relax with the dust, which would be brought in special vehicles with attendants to dispense it impartially. Their position in the battlefield would be in the centre of the conflicting armies and respected by both sides . . .' Nagaraj was relieved to find the pundit in a mood of communication. In order to keep up the good temper, he expressed appreciation of the old man's wide learning. And then, gradually, he came down to this subject, 'Any reference to Narada in the battles?'

'No. He was peace-loving. His gossips led to wars, but he was himself peace-loving and never had a scratch on him.'

'When do we start?' Nagaraj could not help asking.

'Don't be in a hurry. At an auspicious day and time which must come by itself, like a baby after ten months.' The pundit laughed at his joke and Nagaraj was distraught. Soon it would strike four and the old man would complain of failing light. He did not know how to handle this man. He prayed silently to Narada (though he is not a god but a celestial being) for help.

The old man asked, 'Are you praying?'

'Yes, to Narada.'

'He can't help you unless the time comes,' and added, 'All good things must begin at the ripe moment, otherwise they will rot like a plucked unripe fruit. To find the right time, you must have the right time again. An auspicious moment or day must be sought in the almanac only at an auspicious moment to begin with.'

'Auspicious moment to seek an auspicious moment?' Nagaraj exclaimed, unable to understand the idea. It seemed to him an endless quest, like seeing one's reflection standing between two mirrors. 'Perhaps this man will never find the right moment, the reflection in one mirror only reflecting another mirror, and in a hall of mirrors one could go crazy, never being able to find the door. Shall I ask the man to return my money?' He could not pluck up the courage to ask. After another hour's palaver of the same sort he left, sunk in thought. 'I don't care for the hundred rupees thrown away, but this cannot go on forever, I must do something . . .'

Too early to go home (at this hour the harmonium will be going full blast), Lord, help me, or back to Coomar's? Too weary to visit the Boardless again and answer Varma's inane questions, such as why he was coming again after his earlier cup only at two o'clock. 'None of his business to keep count of my cups. I am tired of trudging Ellaman Lane for no purpose, leaving the ledger entries incomplete. But Coomar is very uncomplaining – good fellow; he can't complain, also, because I work free. How can he really? If I accept even ten rupees as salary, I would have to stand before him and seek his permission to go out at his hour, a futile activity in any case. The only useful thing the pundit suggested was to try meditation on the river steps. But I do not know how to meditate. The only subject on which I can meditate is this slippery pundit and his devious ways.'

Unnoticed, his feet turned towards the river steps. He found himself sitting on the last step with his feet in running water. Its cool touch mitigated his agitation. 'I will never see that man again. I am quite sick of him. Everyone thinks he can do what he likes with me, say anything or do anything, little realising that I have assumed a mild attitude deliberately, in order not to hurt others. There was a time when even my father could not check my fiery temper – remember the old Deepavali, when I flung a whole packet of firecrackers into the street gutter simply because he called me . . . I don't remember what. Not a donkey, that is a favourite phrase of Gopu's when he addresses Tim. Some day he is going to hit back, he has already retorted, "What is a donkey's father?", before running away from home. The boy has become soft-headed after marriage! He deserved a better wife. Should not say this. After all, a good girl, though odd looking; something that can't be helped – but she can certainly stop singing, can't she? Now, if what the T.M. said comes through, she will make us the laughing stock of the community. I have not mentioned it to Sita yet. When she comes to know, can't say how she will react. Already she has a secret grouse that the girl takes no interest in the kitchen. It is only a grouse; even if the girl tried, she would not be allowed to touch anything in there except her own dinner plate, and Sita would prefer that she goes back to her harmonium . . .

'Life is getting more and more complex. All that I seek is freedom, peace of mind and scope to write my book. For that I have to depend on others . . . The pundit is probably holding out for more money, having been a gambler all his life. I am going to show that the book will be written without his interference. The story of Narada is known to everyone in our country, even a child knows it. One does not have to be a pundit to talk about Narada. I can do it if I sit down and recollect all the stories my grandmother told me, while she held me down on her lap coaxing me to swallow the rice forced between my lips. Alas, I could not note down anything, naturally; how could one at that age?'

Nagaraj realised his thoughts were wandering wildly, while he had come to the river steps to meditate on Narada. Come what may, he was going to start without wasting further time. He recollected an advice of the librarian (old one or the new one, could not remember) to invent stories of Narada. Excellent idea, that was how the Saint's biography grew and became authoritative literature over a range of a million years, each narrator inventing and adding some stuff, the great sage himself inspiring every story-teller in his own way. 'Invent' was a wrong word: nothing was invented, nothing can occur to the mind out of a vacuum – there must have been a spark of something which was blown up into a flame. 'Oh, Sage!' he murmured as a prayer in tune with the murmur of the leaves overhead and the chirping of birds, 'give me an idea and let it grow and flourish.' After the prayer his mind was easy. He was going to look into the almanac and fix an auspicious time to begin his effort. Before that he must go to Bari and buy a good notebook and ink and pen. Before everything else, discuss it with Sita.

He got up. He must hurry before Bari closed. Within one hour he was at the other end of Market Road and was happy to find Bari's open. That itself was a good sign. Bari came up effusively. 'Why have we not met for months?' he asked, holding out his hand.

'I am not going to touch his hand, it will be sticky or

ink-stained. I have seen him pour ink out of a big bottle into smaller ones for his customers – that was to get more profit than by retailing smaller sealed bottles directly. Profit at any cost is their religion! They are all alike. Coomar's blouse pieces are cut out of unsold saris.' His further reflections were interrupted by the embroidered-shirt-clad Bari offering, 'Just say it, and it is yours. Only yesterday, I was telling Gupta, you know our hardware man, that you never came this way nowadays. Now what can I do for you?'

Nagaraj mentioned his purpose slowly and clearly. 'I want some high-class notebooks for some special high-class work.'

'Go up and fetch the Tower-brand books cleared yesterday from the train,' he said to an attendant standing behind him. He turned to Nagaraj. 'Something special from Sweden, cleared only two days back from the Madras Harbour and landed in a goods train, though I had asked them to send the consignment by passenger train only to save time, but they do not care. I stored them up over there specially with you in mind; didn't want to offer to others than Coomar's, whose stationery, like their silks, have to be in a special class.'

Nagaraj was beginning to think, 'This man has begun his chatter and won't leave me in peace to choose as I like. Why is my life plagued by fellows of this type everywhere? People who talk their heads off, like that pundit . . .' They waited, staring upward at the servant on the ladder, who picked up a handful of books, more than he could hold, and dropped them, and then took a false step and came skidding down the ladder, scattering the books on the floor. 'They look like a mass of flowers in their coloured bindings,' Nagaraj reflected while the servant was nursing his elbows. Bari said, 'Not for the first time. I have told this fool so often not to lift more than he can hold, but he wants to save a second trip, lazy beggar. Hey, Sunil! Get up and go next door for a cup of tea and you will be all right. Get up, get up, don't malinger . . .' He gave him a coin. Sunil straightened himself and went out, limping. Looking after him, Bari commented,

'These days we have to be careful with labour – they are not what they used to be. I had ten fellows here at one time, and when they began to form unions, I reduced my staff. I got this fellow from Aligarh, and I keep him busy so that he has no time to gossip with others on Market Road.'

Nagaraj paid no attention to his talk but picked up a couple of notebooks from the floor, examined them and said, 'This is not what I want. These are account ledgers.'

'The best you can get from Sweden. I ordered them especially with Coomar's in mind.'

'The pages are full of debit and credit columns, in colour. I want a plain notebook for my personal use.'

'Why didn't you say so? You want plain or ruled? How many pages? All the details you must give, otherwise difficult. My philosophy is to give complete satisfaction to my customers. Do you like glazed paper or matt? You must make up your mind. I can't make it up for you – that is my philosophy in business.'

Nagaraj thought, 'Talks too much!' and said aloud, 'I want a very good notebook to write in – '

'Tell me whether bound or unbound, how many pages . . .'

'Nicely bound – '

'Nicely bound? We have a good variety . . .' He turned to the boy, who was just limping in after his tea, and cried, 'Hey, go up and fetch the two-hundred-page Crow-brand.' The boy hesitated, whereupon he cried again, 'Go up and fetch. What do you think I am keeping you for? Go up, and take care, don't imagine I'll give you money for tea again! If you fall, I'll pack you off to Aligarh.' The boy went up the ladder sullenly. Bari glared after him and said, 'Troublesome fellow. Communists have filled them with notions.'

It was nearly seven when Nagaraj decided that he did not like any of the samples shown. He explained, 'I am beginning an important work on Narada . . .'

'Ah, Narada! Great saint, and so practical!' cried Bari. 'How much he has done for the universe!'

'You know him?'

'Who doesn't? Every child in our part of the country can tell his story!'

'Your country?'

'In Aligarh.'

'Yes, you told me that already . . .'

'Every child and adult can tell you the story of that great saint. His temple in our village is very old. We have a Narad festival. Once a year I close this shop and visit the temple for a week. It is our family right to conduct the annual festival . . .'

Nagaraj was thrilled. He had reached the end of a quest, seeing the light at the end of a tunnel. He grasped the other's hand and cried, 'I must see you every day. I need your help.'

'Anything you want. If you want a fountain pen with a thick handle and broad nibs, you will have to wait for a week. To tell you a secret, I am planning to bind special notebooks in Hamilton Bond, partly gilt-edged. I am making up an order of a particular individual whose name I can't reveal, but you can have the first choice. I am making only half a dozen now. I'll have them delivered at your door if you can wait for a week. Ideal paper for Narad.'

'Very good, give it at the earliest.'

'I won't offer it to all and sundry, only to special customers.'

'Thank you. Hamilton Bond is the best, I know.'

'We are the only agents; his signed portrait hangs on the wall of my house. You must come and see it . . .'

Before they bade goodnight to each other, Nagaraj asked, 'Did you say that your boy is from Aligarh?'

'Of course, straight from our village, where my real name is "Basi". Someone typed it as "Bari" in an application and somehow it has stayed . . . As I was saying, that boy is from our village. He stays with me. I do not let him out of my sight.'

'Does he speak about Narada?'

In order to demonstrate, Bari summoned the boy and asked, 'Where do you come from?'

He blinked for a moment and said, 'Gotia.'

'Who is the god in the temple there?'

'Narad Maharaj,' the boy said promtly.

At which Bari said, 'I take him with me to Gotia every year, and I don't let him out of sight anywhere. He can tell you more stories of Narad than any pundit can.'

'Pundits are no good,' Nagaraj said dolefully.

He went back home feeling triumphant. 'I went in the wrong direction and wasted my time, meeting the pundit. I should have come to this end of Market Road instead of Ellaman; I could have written the first chapter by now . . .' He was in such a glow of contentment that he hardly noticed Saroja's harmonium at first, and when he did hear it, he said to himself, 'Let the poor girl go on if it gives her satisfaction. After all, it's some kind of music appealing particularly to Delhi folk, who have also ears, but perhaps different from ours.'

He burst in on Sita while she was starting the evening supper. 'I have happy news. I have found a man who is a treasure house on Narada. From tomorrow I am going to be very, very busy.'

'What do you mean by it?' she asked in rather a matter-of-fact way.

'I'll have to start writing on Narada – '

'Oh, that! It's always Narada – I thought you were going to be the Chairman of the Municipality!'

'Why, do you think Narada is less important?'

'Have you had coffee or do you want some? Some decoction is left.'

He felt piqued at her lack of interest, but told himself, 'She is happy about it but won't exhibit it. Likes to tease me, that's all, an old wife's privilege after decades of married life!' He explained at length about his visit to Bari and about his village god in Aligarh. She was duly impressed and mixed his coffee without any further remark about his obsession.

After coffee he repaired to his seat on the pyol and watched the street in a state of tranquillity, in spite of the harmonium in the background.

Next day, at the end of his work at Coomar's, he went to Bari directly, waited patiently till his closing time, watching his transactions and listening to his remarks, comments and philosophy. When Bari had locked up his shop, Nagaraj followed him to his house at the back of the shop in a side street, an old area known as Sowcarpet, where originally were settled businessmen and moneylenders who had migrated from 'upper India', speaking Hindi and Gujarati and other languages of the North. Bari's was an ancient house, as spacious as Nagaraj's Kabir Street home. It had a hall with old sofas, cushions on the floor, with pictures of gods on the walls in addition to Hamilton of Hamilton Bond. Bari seated him comfortably, offered him tea and fruits and then went in and brought an old volume with dusty edges in a grimy faded binding. 'This is *Narad Puran*, our family heirloom . . .'

They came to an arrangement: Nagaraj to visit him three days in the week, going home with him after the shop. He would read aloud from the book, translate and explain, and Nagaraj to take notes and go home and write it in his own way. 'How should I show my gratitude?'

'You buy the paper for printing the book from me and nowhere else, that must be your promise to me. I can give you white printing, twenty-four or thirty-six pounds as you like, which you won't see anywhere in this part of the world.'

While waiting for Bari to close his shop, Nagaraj kept thinking, 'Although he mentions Narada as being the subject of his ancient book, I'd like him to read out at least ten lines so that I may be sure that the book deals with Narada and not Viswamithra, who was an equally dynamic sage: a warrior king, at one stage, lusting for conquests, but became a sage through fierce meditation. If I wrote about him, I'd not have to depend on Bari or the cards-loving pundit, material could be picked up from the library of my neighbour Sambu himself, who goes on reading all day by his window.' He suddenly asked, 'Bari, what do you think of Viswamithra, who was also a great sage?'

'I know, he is in the Ramayan, but not as great as Narad. We don't have a temple for Viswamithra anywhere.'

'I would like to hear you read your big book a page or two, so that I may enjoy the sound of your language and hear about Narad.'

Bari readily agreed, 'Tomorrow evening we'll go home and read: it is a masterpiece. In our place we treat it as high as Valmiki Ramayan.'

Nagaraj was impressed and sent up an apology to Sage Narada for the sudden lapse on his part. 'Of course, one has to accept Viswamithra's greatness, but now I am committed to writing on Narada. If I succeed, I'll write a second book on Viswamithra, and maybe a whole series to be called 'Sages of India'; quite a lot of material available – there are Seven Sages, who are the progenitors of mankind.'

Eventually Bari persuaded Nagaraj to make a start on the available paper. 'Blue ledger, which is also excellent but not imported. I have got ready some books – you may start on it and later copy it down on Hamilton when the supply comes.' He summoned Sunil and drove him up the ladder to fetch the 'Crow-brand'. The boy asked from the top of the ladder, 'How many?' Bari turned to Nagaraj and repeated the question. While Nagaraj was considering the question, Bari asked, 'How many pages are you going to write?'

Nagaraj did not know, but to end the uncertainty replied promptly, 'One hundred pages first part.'

Bari looked up and shouted, 'Bring two fifty-pages,' adding to Nagaraj, 'When you have used up fifty pages of the notes while you sit up with me, you may use the other fifty for your own composition from the notes.'

While carrying the brown parcel of two fifty-page Crow-brand notebooks, Nagaraj felt he had passed another definite stage towards his mission in life. Next morning after the bath and puja, he wore his ochre robe, took the Crow-brand notebooks into the puja room, said his prayers as usual, placed the notebooks at the pedestal of gods and consecrated them by sprinkling flowers on them. Sita observed his activities but refrained from questioning because of his ochre robe.

At Bari's house next evening, after tea, Bari came to business. He brought along the ancient volume and kept it on its stand, opened the cover and began to read the text in a sing-song voice. While he read the first page, Nagaraj watched anxiously to catch the name 'Narada', to assure himself that the other man was not palming off some other sage. From time to time Bari paused to translate in broken English and Tamil the contents. Nagaraj sat bemused, but the other went on with zest. After listening for a while, Nagaraj ventured to ask, 'How is it there is no mention of Narad yet?'

Bari explained, 'He is not born yet. He won't be born for a long time to come. The poet explains how the universe was created by Brahma from his lotus seat poised on the Navel of the Supreme Lord Vishnu . . . Then comes the deluge. Narad's great-grandfathers and their ancestors have to be born first . . .'

Nagaraj wanted to dispute this theory. He had read that Narad was an immaculate conception, created by the Supreme Lord by a mantra, and sent down to earth and other planets and the galaxy and Milky Way on special missions. Though he could not accept Bari's theory, he let him read on without interrupting him. Ten evenings later Nagaraj found one notebook filled with notes. When he perused the pages on the morning of the eleventh day, sitting calmly on the pyol, he realised that he had been scribbling down chaotically and phonetically whatever had emanated from Bari's throat, who read out in a frenzy in a sort of linguistic cocktail of Hindi, English and Tamil. Nagaraj sat on the pyol in a state of complete abstraction, trying to make out the notes, unmindful of the traffic on Kabir Street. So preoccupied was he that he did not notice the presence of the Talkative Man, who stood below on the road and had to call out 'Nagaraj!' several times before attracting notice.

'Ah, come up and see this,' Nagaraj cried on seeing him, as if a saviour had come.

'What is it? Have you already begun your masterpiece? Or finished it?'

'I am about to begin. Come up and see!'

T.M. came up the steps, saying, 'I am in a hurry but your work seems important. It may be a news item for my paper.' He came up and sat on the pyol, looked through the pages and could not conceal his amusement. 'Looks like planchette writing. I attended a seance once at New Extension where they were trying to contact the dead through a planchette, which scribbled something like this. What exactly is it?'

'Go on, try to read it.'

'I have not the time today, only came to take the scooter from your neighbour – but, anyway, where did you acquire these spirit messages?'

Nagaraj explained, 'Bari translated passages from his book in broken Tamil and pidgin English and sometimes burst into his own lingo – and I took it down as I heard it, phonetically. I do not know what to do now . . . Well, I'll persist; he has the great book. I'll get something out of it in course of time. I have hopes. Tell me, should I write my book in English? I am beginning to doubt . . .'

'Why?'

'I do not know enough grammar.'

'Should make no difference.'

'I thought it would be best in English, to reach the wide world. After all, I want Narada's personality to be understood universally, irrespective of caste, creed, nationality or religion.'

'Excellent idea. For this purpose English is the right language – the only language free from the grammarian's tyranny.'

Nagaraj was pleased. 'Just what I thought. I am happy we think alike.'

After a couple of days Bari resumed his reading, and another Crow-brand notebook was filled in the next few days. Nagaraj had to indent for six more books so that he might begin his composition right away. 'Where shall I sit and write?' was the next question. 'The last room in the third courtyard would be out of reach of all noise, and I hope of the harmonium too!' He told Sita, 'When the sweeper comes, get a room cleaned and ready for me. I'll sit there and write.'

Sita swept the room, spread a mat on the floor and put in an old sloping desk on which one could work squatting on the floor. 'Or do you prefer a chair and table? The only ones in this house are in Tim's room. We had a cane chair but it has a hole and has been in the loft for years waiting to be repaired. Do you want it?'

'What is she driving at?' Nagaraj wondered. 'How can I sit in that cane chair with a hole? Is she taking it all as a joke?' He suppressed his doubts about Sita's intentions and said, 'Our tradition is to squat on the floor and write.'

She was unusually light-hearted today. 'I don't know why she is in this mood . . . This is a solemn occasion.' He knew he sounded ridiculous but could not help blurting out, 'Valmiki must have been sitting down on the ground while composing the Ramayana.'

'But did they have chairs in those days?' Sita asked, laughing slyly.

'Why is she mocking me?' Nagaraj wondered, but replied with due seriousness, 'This is an important work I am beginning, my dear. I have taken so much trouble to collect information . . .'

She modified her tone and asked, seriously now, 'Will it bring you a lot of fame?'

'If people read it.' He was amazed at Sita's concern. He never suspected that she would be interested in his writing. 'After so many years, I'm discovering her,' he thought. 'I have been doing her an injustice, thinking of her only as companion to feed me and look after my comforts.'

CHAPTER 12

He was up at five next morning, violating Sita's edict that he should sleep till seven, and Sita had to get up earlier and adjust her timing too. Nagaraj went through his morning rituals at great speed, bathed, drank his coffee and performed the puja, changed to white dhoti from ochre robes, and was at his sloping desk before seven with his pen poised above the Crow-brand notebook on the desk. He kept saying, 'Sita, you don't bother. I can look after myself.'

'How?' she asked. 'Your mother never taught you even how to mix your coffee.' He had no answer to it, and was reminded of an obscure line of poetry from his college days: 'Men must work and women must weep, although the harbour be moaning.' 'I suppose it can't be helped,' he thought and accepted her services as inevitable. 'We must sleep earlier hereafter, I suppose.' He would have to cut short his relaxation on the pyol after dinner by half an hour. 'Without proper organisation and adjustment, nothing can be achieved,' he kept saying to himself. Aloud, he told Sita, 'This will be only for a few weeks . . .'

'You will complete it?' she asked, and Nagaraj was troubled again by the thought that she was quipping.

He said, 'Not exactly . . .' unable to understand why he had mentioned 'weeks' instead of 'months' or 'years' and he decided to let it rest there, unable to conclude his sentence.

He sat down to it but could not decide what should be the opening lines. 'Once upon a time . . .' was such a handy and sensible beginning for any story in olden days. Now nobody used it; it's a pity that it's considered old-fashioned. How very practical it would be if he could straight away start, 'Once upon a time there was Narada . . .' Critics would sneer, 'Is this writer a thousand years old? Could almost be a contemporary of Narada . . .' He abandoned 'Once upon a time', and was biting the pen to think of a fresh start. He was not familiar with modern literature; his knowledge was confined to texts taught by Professor Kumar, out of which an assortment of quotable lines remained like sediments . . . not much of use for his present purpose. Must have a chat with Sambu, whose library might have some clue. 'Lives of great men remind us that we could make ours sublime . . .' came up to the surface lines. 'Yes, that is true,' he commented, 'but so difficult to write about. Between the card-playing pundit and Bari's muddled translations, so difficult to write . . .'

The literary struggle went on for a week. He constantly pored over his notes, and wrote down in the belief that if you plunged in, the right passage would emerge. He suddenly said to himself, 'Do you think that writers always thought over and then wrote? No sir, just inspiration. What is this thing called inspiration? Something that is churned out of a lot of mental struggle, something that has to be dug out, and at the end it comes out like the spring at the bottom of a well.' This analogy somehow soothed his soul as a piece of discovery, and a clue. 'Plunge straight in and you will come up with a pearl oyster.' So he decided to plunge into 'Once upon a time' and watch for developments. 'One can always erase the first sentence, and put something else in its place to satisfy readers.' So he began briskly, 'Once upon a time all the gods in heaven were agitated . . .' He paused to ask himself, 'What were they agitated about?' He sat thinking for a while and added, '. . . about various things . . . about the state of the universe where Evil was rampant . . .' 'Rampant? I have never used the expression in my life. Must look into a dictionary. Is there one at home? Father used to take out of the cupboard a red-bound dictionary whenever he sat down to help in my lessons. At the Albert Mission they always punished me for my spelling, particularly words like "commit" or "receive". To this day I am never certain "receive" should be "ieve" or "eive"; it does not matter at this stage, but in those days they made me write down the word one hundred times and bring it to the class, otherwise they would make me stand outside the classroom and do it. Awful days! I wonder how I survived it at all. Whenever I had to write an imposition, my father pulled out the red-covered dictionary and noted down in bold letters on a piece of paper "receipt", "knowledge" or whatever it was, so that I might not blunder again . . . But where is the dictionary? Have not seen it for years.' He suddenly called out, 'Sita, Sita, will you come for a moment?' He shouted, 'What happened to the dictionary, a red-bound one, used to be in Father's almirah?'

'Ask your brother, or your lawyer . . .' Nagaraj realised that his brother must have cleaned up the almirah at the partition of property. He remembered that the shelf had contained an assortment of volumes – epics, philosophy, a dictionary, and old schoolbooks – though he never could remember his father spending any time with a book in hand. Would it be practical to write to his brother to ask for the dictionary? Or would it start family complications? 'Fellow is looking friendly these days, why endanger it? Better borrow it from Sambu.'

He had spent two hours before his desk, and realised that between his ruminations and reminiscences his actual pen had run on to only a dozen lines. He looked over his quota for the day and let out a sigh at the ocean of work that lay ahead, and rose.

The next day's effort was no better. Reminiscences did not intrude, but his notes from Bari's reading were puzzling. He did not know how to reduce them all to a cogent, relevant narrative. Nowhere could he find a mention of Narada. But he had hopes that he would appear; bound to appear ultimately beyond an enormous jungle of verbiage. After all, the old volume had on it the title *Narad Puran*. He made sure that it was so by asking Bari to read aloud the title page every day as a routine formality at the commencement of each session. That was enough to convince him that the book dealt with the right theme.

Studying his notes, he often came across the phrase 'the Great Egg', which was rather obscure at first. But repeated reading produced visions of an enormous egg spanning earth and heaven. It was the womb of the universe, if he understood it correctly. When it burst . . . who could burst it, actually? Was it to be split with an enormous axe? Questions which had no answer in any form. The egg floated on an enormous sea among giant waves in total darkness. Where was the sun then? That, too, had to wait for the egg to be split. Impossible to conceive the size of an egg which could contain the solar system itself. Nagaraj, sitting at his sloping desk, rewrote it reverently, brushing aside his own doubts. It would be sacrilegious to question too much. Old texts mentioned the egg, and they must have had good reason to say so; the chronicles were inspired and the chroniclers were rishis, beings who knew what they were saying. If they mentioned Egg they must have meant it. So he accepted the idea, and integrated it in his own narrative, which read something like the following: 'Once upon a time, a great egg floated on the sea in pitch darkness. The sun was not created yet. It was still within the egg . . .' He read and re-read his composition and commented to himself, 'Not at all bad for a start. I can polish it later with someone's help; who is the best person to look over this? I don't know, perhaps such a person has not come out of the great egg yet.' He allowed himself a heretical smile at the notion, but checked himself immediately. He kept scribbling down strictly till the closing hour signalled by the hall clock striking nine, when he got up with relief. The next day's notes were all about the unmitigated all-enveloping darkness, through which no sort of outline was visible.

Thus it went on, day after day. He spent three evenings with Bari, which provided him with enough material for four days. Even after filling a couple of Crow-brand notebooks he was unable to assess his work or understand what he was doing. He could have no objective view of his own composition, but went on spinning his yarn, groping in the darkness with the tremendous Egg still intact, wafting in the ocean. When it burst Creation would begin, and surely Narada would be the first to emerge.

Sita asked him one morning when he came out of the writing room, 'How is it coming?'

And he had to confess, 'God's ways are inscrutable.'

She asked, 'What do you mean by that?'

'I can't explain,' he said.

And she looked at him and murmured, 'No one compels you to write.'

'It will all be child's play if the wife is helpful,' he thought as he made his way to the pyol. He was happy that he was at his mission, but he was unhappy at the same time at his wife's sarcasm.

Saroja noticed Nagaraj early one morning, and asked, 'Why are you up so early, Uncle?'

Nagaraj exclaimed, 'I have a lot of work; in the calm hours of early morning, one can write better and get through a lot of work easily . . .' He had just finished his quota of writing and was moving towards the street, and Saroja was clutching a bundle of clothes, passing from her room towards the bath in the backyard. He felt he should say something to her. 'Oh, so much to wash!'

She said, 'Yes, most of these are Tim's,' and then she added, 'If I also get up early, I could wash all this early in the morning . . .'

'Why should you get up so early? You should take it easy.'

'No, Uncle. My problem is that I too want a lot of time to finish my work and be free to practise.'

He appealed to Sita some time later, 'Saroja is threatening

to get up early. Please tell her to stay in bed as late as possible. If her harmonium is played . . .'

'You can't stop her from playing. After all, she plays only in her room. And you will be in the courtyard.'

'But her harmonium pursues me even there.'

'Shut the door.'

'It becomes dark.'

'Switch on the light.'

He realised that she was teasing him. 'What has come over this woman?' he asked himself. 'Of late she is treating my writing as a joke.' He suppressed, as usual, his inner voice. 'Please advise her . . .'

'About what?'

'To sleep, and not play her harmonium. I wouldn't mind what she does after the clock strikes nine.'

'When I try to keep you from rising before seven, you don't care.'

'How can I sleep till seven and write?'

'Even before you started all this, it was difficult to hold you down.'

'Why are you talking about me now? We were discussing Saroja.' Their domestic talk was carried on in the kitchen, which was away from the traffic routes of the house and assured them privacy. Sita refused to interfere. 'I have got on with her well, so far. I don't want to spoil it.'

Saroja got up early next day and, after allowing an interval for Nagaraj to finish his bath, occupied the bath shed, beat her washing on the granite slab and was ready for the day, just when Nagaraj was warming up to his theme. Of late his notes were very unclear. After a lot of cosmic egg and darkness the world was submerged in a deluge. The deluge and its effects occupied a whole notebook. He felt a little annoyed with the old chroniclers, at their lack of economy. Too much detail, too slow. 'Why don't you get on with the subject and bring Narada in? After all, I am writing about Narada, not about floods and darkness . . .'

But there was no way of speeding up, partly due to the old

chroniclers' ways, and partly due to Saroja's early-morning activities. Nagaraj could not keep his mind on the subject. Saroja beat wet clothes on a stone noisily, and until the thunderous pit-pat of washing ceased his thoughts remained scattered. When the disturbance ceased, he heaved a sigh of relief and tried to resume, but the respite was short-lived. It lasted only till she passed through to her room, where she began to hum film tunes while grooming herself before her looking glass. After that came the harmonium. While holding the pen over paper Nagaraj realised that it would not move. His whole attention was only on the harmonium, following and suffering every single note. Not more than a few lines of incoherence could be scribbled. He sat firmly until the clock chimed nine, and rose with a sense of frustration. Thereafter he sat on the pyol, brooding, until eleven, when he went into the dining room and remained gloomy throughout the meal. Sita guessed what was troubling him. She refrained from questioning or commenting on his state of mind. He dressed as usual before his oval mirror and went out. While he was passing the market gate, Jayaraj hailed him. Nagaraj could not ignore him. Jayaraj enquired, 'I have marked you absent in the attendance register. What's the matter? Every day I wait for you to come and wake me. I see you rarely.' Nagaraj explained his literary preoccupations these days and the altered timetable. Jayaraj congratulated him and wished him fame and fortune. Nagaraj was preoccupied. Jayaraj said, 'You don't look happy. Why do you write, if it makes you sad?'

'It's a hard task.'

'Then stop it. Who compels you to go on? Your wife?'

'Oh, no. She won't interfere, that's the trouble. She is aloof.'

'I don't understand your complication. She must have her own reason.'

Nagaraj passed on. At Kanni's he held out his hand mechanically for betel leaves. Kanni took notice of his glum mood but was too busy serving others to enquire. Nagaraj reached Grove Street, wondering if he should not shift in the morning to some other place – for instance, the temple hall or corridor, which would be quiet. The old watchman could be persuaded to open the side door and find a quiet corner for him. He brightened up at the idea, gloated over it and attained peace of mind to some extent. In such a tranquil state, he greeted Coomar and others and went straight to his seat and picked up the ledgers and was lost in the columns.

The crowd and bustle dispelled his gloom and he could forget for the time being the pains of composition and the harmonium music of Saroja. Tim seemed to be completely out of it all: he left home early, came back to eat in his wife's company, and left again, came home, threw a word at his uncle and aunt, shut himself in his room and left again – seen off by his wife, the only time when the harmonium ceased. 'I don't mind the harmonium, have got used to it, but not in the morning. Saroja should not rise with the sun . . .' At home, while Sita gave him his coffee in the kitchen, he explained his idea to move to the temple for writing. She said at once, 'Unsound. When you are not able to find silence in your own home, how can you find it in the temple?'

'Only the side door will be opened.'

'It'll make no difference. Worshippers don't care whether the side door or the main door is opened, they will pour in and sound the bells and chant and sing, and shout, worse than the harmonium. No, no, it won't work.'

'Then I have no salvation?'

'I don't know,' she said with undue seriousness. 'You should wear your ochre and plug your ears with cotton wool.'

'Why both?' he asked.

'Ochre will keep people away and cotton wool will keep out all sound.'

He studied her face to find out if she was serious. But she turned away to attend to some work.

Next morning, as usual, he wore the ochre robe in the prayer room. Normally he would change to white clothes after prayer, before going into his work room. Today he crossed the courtyard in the ochre drape and sat down in it at his writing desk. He picked up his notebooks and uttered a brief invocation to Saraswathi, the goddess of learning and enlightenment. He looked over the notes, the source for today's composition. Still the universe was under water, the skies were dark, and it rained without respite. He shivered at the picture of total gloom and soaking dampness with no living organism in sight, under enormous pitch-black clouds. He recollected that years ago a freak monsoon had brought four days of continuous rain in Malgudi. The damp and darkness were depressing; one felt paralysed. He remembered all schools were closed, all shops, and the streets were flooded. All signs of life and movement ceased. In that darkness human outlines were lost. Street dogs were drowned and carried off into storm drains. They said that the Sarayu was rising and would soon submerge the town, and wash it away without a trace. Four days the rains had lashed. Now he read in his notes that the great deluge and storm lasted thousands of years without count. Nagaraj shuddered at the picture of it and felt grateful to be living at the present time. He was reflecting on this gloomy scene, wondering how much of it would be relevant to his theme and how to reduce twenty-five pages of gloom to a few lines in his composition and relate it to the main theme. It was an agonising exercise because it went on and on when he tried to write it down, repeating the gloom, downpour and the accompanying discomforts and black moods he had experienced during the great rains of Malgudi when young.

Now Nagaraj had ten notebooks full. After digesting these he would resume the sessions with Bari; he would begin the next and after that another session and another; thus it might go on how long? Seemed indefinite and he felt worried about it; this could not go on forever, early-rising was getting on his nerves . . . While his mind was grappling with these problems, the harmonium was blaring away. He covered his ears with his palms, halting his fountain pen, and remembered Sita's advice (ever the wisest counsellor) about plugging the ears with cotton wool. He had searched for cotton wool yesterday, but not a shred available in the house; he had poked his hand into every almirah and box and shelf, but no use. Finally he requested Sita, 'Ask the lady next door if she has a piece of cotton wool in her first-aid box.'

Sita laughed and said, 'We could if you had a cut or bruise but not for your present purpose. We can't mention the reason.'

'But what shall I do tomorrow morning? I'll wear the ochre, but you have also told me to plug my ears.'

'Tomorrow get it at the medical store.'

'But I can't do it so early in the day.' She gave him no answer, and he realised now that he had blundered in not thinking of cotton wool earlier. 'After all, for a rupee a whole roll is available; it would have lasted for over a year . . .' he thought with regret.

He simply could not stand the harmonium sound any more. He felt unusually irritated, got up abruptly intending to knock or bang on Saroja's door and tell her, 'Stop your music for the next hour or two. Otherwise things will be bad for you.' When he went up to knock on her door violently, he found it open; she was sitting on the floor with her harmonium. When he stood in the doorway, mustering courage to give her a proper talking down, she herself said, thinking that he had come to appreciate her music, 'Uncle, I am trying a new song I listened to on the radio last night. Do you like it?'

Nagaraj felt knocked out, could speak neither the truth nor untruth. While he was hesitating she said, 'Oh! You have come in your puja dress. I know you won't talk when you are wearing it, and won't be disturbed. I hope you don't find my music a disturbance.' He just attempted a benign smile, took advantage of his ochre not to speak, turned round and went back to his writing. He was haunted by her eager face, alien looking, seeking appreciation. Sita told him later, 'Let that poor girl play her harmonium, why should you mind it? You are sitting far away in the third court.'

'But the harmonium sound is everywhere . . .'

'You are exaggerating; your ancestors have anticipated all this trouble and built these walls two feet thick.'

'But I have to get on with my writing.'

'And Saroja has to get on with her music. What else can she do? She doesn't know what to do in the kitchen, she has nothing to do all day.'

'Why don't you train her in household work?'

'It's not her line. Anyway, let her actual mother-in-law give her the training. Why should I? However, if she shows any interest, I am ready!'

He spent the next afternoon visiting Dr Velu of Velu Medical Hall on Market Road. It was about five o'clock and the doctor was not yet to be seen. A late lunch followed by a prolonged siesta always delayed his evening visit to his clinic, and patients were sitting, lounging and lying on benches and steps and floor in various stages of ill health. He was reputed to have the healing touch and a crowd always waited and swarmed around when he arrived on his scooter in his striped cotton suit and knitted tie and hat. Such meticulous dressing took time and he always arrived late, resulting in a swarm of patients jostling in his clinic.

When he arrived, a servant held his scooter and took it away, and when he stepped in with the stethoscope dangling from his neck, he was practically mobbed by patients following him with a babble of complaints. He stood before them, held up his arms, and said, 'Go back to your seats and stay there. Come one by one when I call you.' The doctor took his seat in the hall with a final threat, 'If you are going to be like this I'll see no one today but leave immediately. I will go out on my round of visits.' The mob withdrew. The doctor sounded a bell. A cadaverous tall man wearing thick glasses materialised, who wore a khaddar jibba and white Gandhi cap. The doctor waved a finger, and the man withdrew and went to the waiting hall, looked at Nagaraj and beckoned to him, in recognition of his special standing as a Kabir Street citizen. At the sight of him the doctor rose and advanced with his hand held out. 'Nagaraj, it seems a hundred years since I saw you. What brings you now? Are you keeping well? What's wrong with you today?'

'For a very insignificant reason I have come. I can wait.'

'No, I'll attend to the old friend first. Others can wait, the usual running noses, throat, stomach ache and what not. I hope to go on giving relief with God's grace. Where I feel helpless I send them on to Dr Natwar, who has a polyclinic on Mempi Road with all sorts of gadgets, but he is expensive, I can't send him all my patients, who are poor and illiterate. I don't charge more than two rupees for any prescription . . . The tongue is loosened when old friends meet. Now, what is the matter with you? I am at your service.'

'Nothing important,' Nagaraj said, feeling that he had blundered in coming here for mere cotton wool and that he should give some reasonable explanation. 'I didn't wish to worry over a small matter, but actually I have come to ask if you can give me a little cotton.'

'What for? Any injury or cut?'

'Oh, no, it's something very minor. Of late I feel some sort of noise in the ear, and I wonder if a plug of cotton wool will help.'

'What sort of noise? Do you hear a humming or hissing? Any pain while it lasts? Is it intermittent or continuous?' The doctor came over and tugged his ear and peered in with a torch. 'Any dizziness accompanying the hissing?'

'It's something very minor, of no importance, nothing to worry – '

'You are not to come to conclusions. It's a doctor's business. If you read the medical literature on the subject you will see that there are a hundred causes for noise in the ear. We must assume it is a serious symptom and eliminate the cause. After all, there may be nothing except wax.'

'Yes, yes,' agreed Nagaraj. 'I have frequently taken out wax.'

'Never do that!' cried the doctor in alarm. 'If you injure

the tympanum it will affect the brain.' Nagaraj shuddered and remained silent. Everything he said seemed wrong. He was getting a little nervous. He had never thought of his health. Now this doctor's face, held so close and with an expression of being about to pronounce a dreadful verdict, unnerved him. The doctor was asking, 'When did you check your blood pressure last?'

Nagaraj promptly replied, 'About a month ago.'

'What was the reading?'

'Normal.'

'Urine? E.C.G.?'

Though he did not know what E.C.G. meant Nagaraj replied, 'Normal, normal.'

'Who is your doctor?'

'At Madras, related to our family.'

'Is he good?'

'Top-class physician with a lot of practice and a nursing home too . . .' Nagaraj felt it would be impossible to invent further answers to ward off the doctor's interest in him, and feared the doctor would next stretch him on a table and pronounce something dreadful. He got up abruptly saying, 'So many are waiting, I'll be back later,' and started.

The doctor said, 'Wait, wait . . .' He hastily scribbled on a pad, tore off the slip and gave it to him. 'Tomorrow go to Natwar's polyclinic and lab and show this. They will test you and give a report. See me with the report; I'd like to have the latest results.'

Nagaraj fled from the place. 'What evil power inspired me to see the man today! He would have sent me home on a stretcher if I had stayed longer with him!'

On the way he stopped at Ganesh Stores and asked, 'Have you cotton?'

'What cotton?'

'Just ordinary cotton.'

'For what?' asked the shop man.

'Why is everyone so fussy about cotton? What a hard thing to come by!' he thought, and said, 'For this and that, you know! Just simple cotton wool which is applied to wounds and stuffed into ears if there is pain.'

'We don't sell that kind of cotton.'

'Then what kind of cotton do you sell?'

'We don't, but we have these.' He produced a tin box and took out of it a handful of wicks. 'Wicks for oil lamps, especially gods'!'

Nagaraj examined a sample and said, 'Give me a handful.' They were all twisted cotton. He said to himself, 'I could untwist and fluff them out again . . .' He walked home through the evening crowd on Market Road, sunk in thought, saying to himself, 'Thank God I left the doctor in good time, thank God that He gave me the sense to get away in good time. Narrowly escaped.'

At home he did not mention his visit to the doctor, and tore to shreds the slip of paper the doctor had given for the pathologist. Otherwise Sita was likely to take the doctor's advice seriously and nag him to go in for the report. She had a holy faith in doctors and would have become hysterical about his health. He said, 'Managed to find some sort of cotton after all. Tomorrow I can plug my ears and write without any disturbance.'

Sita snatched the little package from his hand. 'The very thing I wanted. I promised to the gods in the temple to light a hundred wicks. Did I tell you?' She sounded very pleased.

'I can always read your mind,' he said, looking very clever. 'I'll bring you more,' he said.

'This will be enough now.'

'But I want a small quantity now.'

'What for?'

'It's your suggestion. I'll plug my ears as you advised.'

She looked horrified and held the packet away from him. 'What an evil notion! To misuse God's lamp-wicks! I never thought you would stoop so low. It's a sin to misuse God's wicks . . .'

'Where did you read this? In which shastra? You can't

appropriate my hard-won cotton!' But as usual he swallowed his words without further argument.

Next day's writing was jerky and chequered. His notes were stagnating at the stage of Cosmology and Cataclysm, without a trace of creation. He found it difficult to use his notes and organise his essay, worrying at the back of his mind what all this had to do with his theme, with a recurring suspicion that Bari was deluding himself with that ancient volume in Rajasthani or some such language; he was in the throes of composition, in a wilderness of doubts and misgivings – not only about the material and its validity but a fundamental harrowing doubt about his competence to write at all! 'What evil genius impelled me to undertake this task? What conceit? Waste of time. Ages since I sat on the pyol with a free mind. Coomar is tolerant, even though I am not giving enough attention to his accounts . . .'

With all the self-criticism on one side, he was still struggling to whip the pen on, not having the heart to stop it. But it was a torment. Into this turmoil and confusion butted the harmonium mercilessly. He flung down the pen and covered his ears. Still the noise persisted and it was agonising. 'I must have committed the worst sins in my previous life to have to hear this now. If I could have barricaded my ears with cotton wool, even with just a wisp of it, I could have mitigated my misery. But cotton? What has happened to all the cotton in the world? Seems more difficult to get than diamonds. To add to all this, Sita with her notions of the sacredness of cotton wicks. At least a couple of wicks could have helped. But she has deprived me of even that relief! Bad woman, unhelpful . . . No, I should not think of her thus. All day she slogs for my comforts . . .'

Next day he started his routine, but dispensing with the ochre cloth which he felt inhibited him since he had to observe total silence while wearing it. Today he was determined to go on with his writing whatever might happen. If disturbed he would go and tell Saroja to shut up. For this his ochre would be an impediment. So he wore a white dhoti as a sort of war preparation.

Just as he feared, the attack came. His struggle to concentrate and progress towards something relevant and sensible was thwarted at the start itself. He had hardly written two lines when his pen jerked and criss-crossed the page involuntarily, driven by a sudden blast of noise from the harmonium. He made up his mind to act. He pushed away his desk and rose to his feet resolutely. He was going to tell her, 'This must stop now,' unambiguously.

Sita had a glimpse of him from her kitchen door as he dashed past with the pen still in his grip, but refrained from asking any question. The moment he appeared at the doorway, Saroja said, 'Oh, Uncle, you are not wearing your ochre dress, and now I can talk to you, and you will speak. I want to try a new piece. I want to know how you like it. It goes like this.' She tapped the keys of her harmonium and read out of a piece of paper, musically, the opening lines of a song which said, 'At midnight I am thinking of you, at dawn I think of you . . .' It seemed all right at dawn and noon, but at midnight? It didn't sound innocent enough. Probably it had a double meaning, in which composers of film songs excelled. He felt a little shy to stand there and listen to such a song from a daughter-in-law of the family. While he was squirming and preparing to get away, the words were drowned in the harmonium noise. 'Thank God the harmonium has no tongue,' he thought, and attempted to sneak away. She stopped the harmonium and said, 'Uncle, you are going away? There are four more stanzas . . .' Nagaraj did not know how to escape. The fury which drove him here from his writing room had evaporated. He did not even remember the strong words he had rehearsed in his room. All that seemed important was to get away before the girl could compel him to utter an appreciative word. While the girl was still singing he slinked away, pretending to have heard a knock on the street door.

He realised that it was going to be impossible to tell the girl to stop. While sitting down to lunch, he whispered to Sita, 'You must come to my rescue. I simply cannot write a single sentence unless Saroja mends her ways. Tell her – '

'Why should I? You do it. I saw you cross the courtyard as if you were going to pick up and smash her harmonium.'

He was pleased that Sita could note his fury and understand that he was not effete. If he was roused, nothing could hold him back. 'Sita should not conclude that I am a smiler at all times. After all the years with me, it's a pity she is beginning to understand me only now.'

The lunch concluded in profound silence. He realised that he would never get any help from Sita. He began to suspect that she enjoyed the harmonium music and Saroja's foolish songs. 'No wonder Sita wants it to go on.' She herself used to play the harmonium once but had to abandon the dreadful instrument when his mother, who had governed the family with a firm hand, advised her that in a crowded family it was unseemly for a girl to isolate herself and practise music.

Nagaraj sat on the plank jutting out of Jayaraj's shop, explained his predicament and sought advice. Jayaraj was busy cutting and nailing frames and could only say, 'Why should you mind? After all, it is music, and when the walls of a home resound with music, prosperity will come.'

Nagaraj said, 'I don't care for prosperity but only quiet for writing.'

Jayaraj persisted. 'But music! It's good for a home.'

'But this isn't music.'

'How can you say so? After all, she has learnt from a master in Delhi and knows what she is doing. Do you think that her father will have spent his time and money for nothing? How can you say it can't be music? You have no ear for music, that's the trouble. After all, this is no family problem; the real problem in a family is different. Take my case. I feel the curse of age . . can't go on forever like this . . . hammering nails on picture frames, can't see the nail head but hit my thumb often, but my sons don't care, they don't even peep in to see what is what . . .'

He went on elaborating his family problems and Nagaraj concluded it would be no use consulting Jayaraj. He asked why he should not give up framing and concentrate on his camera profession. Jayaraj replied, 'Everyone possesses a smuggled camera, and my profession is dwindling . . .' The smuggling of Japanese cameras was his favourite theme; before he could go on elaborating that subject, Nagaraj wanted to leave, realising that Jayaraj was unusually dense.

Nagaraj felt that he was born in an unsympathetic world, unsuspected by him all these days. He decided that he would have to think deeply and find a solution himself. 'God helps those who help themselves,' he reminded himself as he walked away from Jayaraj towards the Sari Centre. Turning into Grove Street, he felt revived. The old lime-washed building in the shade of the margosa tree and the crowd of women passing in and out seemed to him a different world altogether. 'God helps those who help themselves,' kept drumming in some corner of his mind. He nodded to Coomar, lounging on his bolster, talking to a group of customers, mainly women and their escorts, quite a motley. On the fringe were silk weavers and yarn merchants waiting for an audience. Nagaraj genially nodded to Coomar and passed on to his seat, suppressing an impulse to enquire of Coomar if he believed in 'God helps those who help themselves', and if so what it meant and why God wanted to wait till the poor fellow helped himself, and was it fair on God's part? And if the help was not superfluous at this stage? His mind seethed with these metaphysical questions as he sat down in his chair and picked up the day book and cash vouchers. He felt more tranquil in this textile crowd and the sight of smug Coomar on his throne holding his court. The solidity of existence seemed restored for the time being; Narada and harmonium and all the travails in an unhelpful home receded into the background, although somewhere a corner of his brain was repeating, 'God helps . . . etc.'

After his duties at Coomar's were done, he rose to go, putting away the account books. On the way out he threw a paternal farewell smile at Coomar, who was still busy in his court with a different set of courtiers and audience. He checked himself from uttering the 'God helps' formula. But later in the evening he had full scope to discuss the subject with Bari, whom he had to join for the evening study that day. Bari offered him his usual seat and was busy wrapping stationery and pencils for his customers. When he was free, Nagaraj asked, 'Bari, you are a philosopher. Will you tell me if you believe God helps those who help themselves?'

Without a moment's pause, he replied, 'That's my philosophy, otherwise do you think I could have developed this business? Tell me.' He looked so convinced of the basis of his existence that Nagaraj himself prayed secretly, 'God, please help me to help myself for a start. I do not know how to. It reminds me of an auspicious moment to start searching for an auspicious moment.' While Bari was rushing along with his reminiscences, Nagaraj followed his words to some extent while he was addressing his own prayer to God. Bari was just saying, 'Hamilton Bond sole agency would not have come to us without God's help . . .'

'How did you gain that favour?' Nagaraj asked.

'How?' asked Bari. 'By God's grace, of course. My father got Hamilton's signed portrait, which you still find in my home.'

They walked to Bari's house for the reading.

The moment Nagaraj appeared before him with effusive words of welcome on his lips, Gopu, sitting cross-legged on the pyol with a jute handbag at his side, just said, 'Idiot,' and kept looking at him without further speech. Nagaraj was puzzled and could only ask, 'Who?' Gopu repeated, 'Idiot.' This time Nagaraj did not question but thought, 'Why is he calling me "idiot"? Should I not turn round and ask, "What is an idiot's brother?"' He just said, 'Sita has gone out to see her sister, who has arrived from Ceylon.' Gopu ignored this information. Nagaraj hoped he would not be called 'idiot' again and wished he could plug his ears with cotton wool, though it was hard to find.

Gopu had arrived earlier and, finding the house locked, was a little puzzled, never having seen this house locked before; he hesitated on the step with his jute bag in hand. At that moment the engineer emerged from the last house, obviously just starting for the bar. 'Hallo! brother of brother,' he cried cheerily while passing, and Gopu wished he could hide his head somewhere. The engineer stopped to say, 'You are welcome to stay with me, only I am wifeless – but not a widower.'

Gopu was afraid of drunkards and just said, 'I will wait here.'

'The lady went away in the morning,' the engineer said, and passed on.

Gopu said, 'I am not going to ask where is Tim. It is useless to ask you.'

'Yes, yes,' said Nagaraj weakly, feeling that some agreement might propitiate him.

Gopu said, 'Two solid persons, a husband and wife living in your care, leave the house and you don't bother about it. Two solid persons just disappear, vanish into thin air, and you ask no question and have no answer.'

'No, no, I saw them go, but I could not ask questions.'

'Why? What choked your throat? Were you unable to speak?'

'Yes, in a way, you see, I had hardly settled down to my puja.'

'So? You didn't have the curiosity to ask, "Where are you going?" when you see someone in the house go out bag and baggage!'

'Yes, I wanted to ask, but I was wearing the ochre robe – '

'Ochre robe! That's another thing in your mad scheme.'

'You won't understand,' said Nagaraj within himself. 'You'll understand only gobar gas and cattle refuse,' but said aloud, 'I watched them pack up, I watched them go, but I told myself, "Let them. How far can they go, after all?" They did not know that I watched, did not understand that I had been very watchful, ever since the moment Tim cornered me with a sudden remark when I was coming from the bathroom, no, when I was going in . . .'

Gopu listened with an air of resignation. People passing along the street paused to listen to their conversation but resumed their course when the brothers also paused in their talk.

Gopu said, 'Should we sit here for the whole street to listen to what we say? Can't we go in?'

'Oh, yes, of course, I have a key. Sita took away one and gave me the duplicate. We could not find the duplicate at first, and she became impatient.'

'All right, open the door, let us go in,' said Gopu. 'I do not want to gather a crowd to listen to us. This is not a public meeting,' he said in a surly tone.

'It can't be,' Nagaraj said nervously, feeling that the best course would be to agree with whatever Gopu said. 'I am afraid Sita won't be back soon. She made some food and left it for the night; I think we can manage. If we had known you were coming . . .' Nagaraj said, opening the door.

'Oh shut up, more important things to talk about,' said Gopu, following him into the house.

'About what?' Nagaraj asked with an air of innocence. He wanted the subject of Tim to be delayed as long as possible. He knew he was exasperating the other, but he told himself, 'What have I to say to him? I only saw them leave, that is all I know, not more than what Gopu knows, but he bullies me like a lawyer, what is the use?' He said, 'No wonder you feel anxious, but no need, I know where he is.'

'Where?' asked Gopu anxiously.

'Why are you so excited? You used to say that you have friends who inform you of all that happens here – '

'Oh!' Gopu groaned in despair. 'We don't have to discuss that now. How am I to make you stick to the point?'

'Which point?' asked Nagaraj, still dodging the subject. They were sitting on the hall bench. Gopu changed his tactics. 'Come on, tell me from the beginning what happened . . .' in a conciliatory tone.

Nagaraj appreciated the change of tone and decided to talk without dodging, but he did not know where to begin. He remained brooding, searching for the right opening line. 'Gopu wants it all from the beginning.' It began with Narada, of course, inevitably. 'You see, I have to go on with Narada . . .'

'I know your obsession, but what has it to do with Tim? We are talking about Tim, if you don't mind . . .'

'Of course, of course. The problem was no cotton wool was to be found anywhere. I began to wonder what had happened to all the cotton wool in the world.'

'Did you say cotton wool? What did Tim have to do with cotton wool? Did he plan to indulge in the cotton business? It is ruinous. I know speculators who have become beggars.'

'Yes, I know. Even Coomar once tried it but withdrew swiftly when he lost ten thousand in one bid. It's a treacherous business, really, and you are right.'

Gopu gritted his teeth and said, 'Yet, knowing it, you allowed him to play with fire. What sort of guardian are you? To think that the fool prefers you!'

Nagaraj felt it safer to let the other continue in his notion than correct him. To mention that he sought cotton bits to seal his ears against his daughter-in-law's music might not be a good policy. He listened quietly while Gopu went on fulminating against the cotton market, at last conceding, 'Left to himself, I knew he would come to grief in some such way.'

'Thank God, you are not calling him an unleashed donkey. If you call him that again I can't say what he might do.'

Realising that he couldn't get anything out of Nagaraj if he spoke roughly, Gopu swallowed the remarks that came uppermost and asked in a gentle tone, 'Did he have nothing to say while leaving?'

'He might have spoken to Sita – not to me, as he knew when I wore the ochre robe – '

Gopu did not allow him to continue but just asked, 'On the previous day, did words pass between you?'

'I was going for my bath, he came out of his room and blocked my path saying, "Why did you go away while my wife was explaining her song and wanted to sing it to you?" I told him, "There was someone at the door," and he just said, "It is an insult and she wants to go away from here"; that's all he said and he left next morning while I was wearing the ochre robe.'

'You and your robe!' said Gopu severely. 'Has Sita no voice in all this?'

'Of course, he told her the same thing, and I had difficulty in convincing Sita that I did not mean to insult. Sita was unhappy, you know how much she dotes on him.'

'Oh, stop! Why could you not listen to that poor girl's song? Have you no ear, have you no courtesy or feeling?

Everyone says that she sings so well. In Delhi she gives public performances . . .'

'True, true,' said Nagaraj, and commented within himself, 'Yes, possible here also, but for the cotton shortage,' while Gopu was completing his sentence, 'You go on saying "True, true," God knows what you mean by it.'

'She is . . . ' Nagaraj began, and was not sure what to say. Gopu gave up his attempt to carry on a cogent conversation with his brother and just asked, 'Where are they now? At least tell me that clearly.'

'I have my own source of information. Not as ignorant as you think. The Talkative Man in Number One wanders all over the town and keeps an eye on everyone. He told me that Tim is in Kismet.'

Gopu looked horrified. 'How can you tell me that so casually? Have you no feeling of any sort? Kismet! How could you let him go there with his wife?'

'I hear that they have given him an outhouse to live in with his family.'

'What for? Did Tim desert his home and parents in order to end up in a tavern? Did he marry only to keep a wife in a tea-house?'

'No, they are paying him a salary, and also to his wife for her music.' The more Nagaraj spoke the more excited Gopu became, and in his rage jumped up and gripped Nagaraj by his shoulder. Nagaraj felt panicky. In his boyhood he was thrashed by his brother; would he do it again now? He prayed that Sita would appear miraculously and save him from physical harm. Seeing Gopu's face at close quarters he noted mentally, 'He has greying stubble on his chin and upper lip. Won't he shave at least when he comes into town? These rustics don't shave regularly whereas I can't show my face outside unless . . .' Gopu was shouting, 'What have you to say? Silence is no answer. I'll go to a court to get custody of my son . . .'

Nagaraj said, wriggling out of his grip, 'He is twenty-one and may declare that he likes to be where he is.'

Gopu loosened his grip and was in tears from the strain of talking to Nagaraj, and Nagaraj also felt moved. In the midst of his rage Gopu wondered how to classify his brother – whether as a moron or a crafty intriguer always avoiding the main issue on principle. He went back to his seat while Nagaraj said to himself, 'Almost what Cain did to Abel,' remembering suddenly his weekly Bible lessons at Albert Mission High School. Observing his silence, Gopu concluded that he had taught him a lesson. They remained silent and Nagaraj suddenly said, 'I do not know how to make coffee. Shall we adjourn to the Boardless, if you don't mind the walk?'

'Oh, God!' Gopu cried, holding his head. 'Coffee be damned.'

Nagaraj said, 'Sita has made some food; it must suffice for both of us, if you feel hungry. You are too excited today, unnecessarily anxious about Tim. I have never seen you like this. I fear you are famished. If you ate, you would feel calmer. As I told you, there's enough for two; Sita always prepares liberally, always believing some extra demand would come unexpectedly – if not a guest, at least some poor soul at the door – never turns away anyone even if it is midnight.'

Gopu totally resigned himself, realising the impossibility of carrying on any useful talk with Nagaraj about Tim. He said in a quiet voice, as if surrendering to the fate that had thrown him in the company of a man like Nagaraj, 'All right, let us eat.'

Nagaraj cried, 'Ah, that is the right spirit!' and became fussy. He told his brother, 'First change and have a wash.' He ceremoniously threw open the door of Tim's room with, 'Back to your old room – we will talk about Tim tomorrow first thing. Sita will also be here. Now eat and rest.' Gopu felt helpless. He sat down to his supper when Nagaraj laid the plates, called him in, seated him on a silver-studded plank and served his food with many apologies for its inadequacy. 'The food is cold, but I do not dare to light a fire . . .'

'Never mind,' said Gopu and ate in silence. After food,

Nagaraj brought him a mug of water to rinse his mouth and wash his fingers. When they went back to the hall bench he produced the silver plate with betel leaves and nut. Chewing, a great state of tranquillity befell them, and this was the right moment for Sita to return. She was relieved to find the atmosphere so calm, having been worrying all along how Gopu would react to Tim's departure. She greeted her brother-in-law formally, with respect, avoiding the subject of Tim, and passed in. When she came out of her room, Nagaraj said, 'We have eaten.'

'It was good,' said Gopu.

Sita said, 'Had I known you were coming . . .'

Gopu merely repeated, 'It was all right.'

'Have you had anything to eat?' asked Nagaraj.

'My sister has come from Ceylon and we had our food.' She turned round and went into the kitchen, beckoned to Nagaraj and whispered, 'Was it all right? Should you not have told me he was coming?'

'I never knew.'

She said, 'I found this postcard on the window sill. It must have been lying there for two days, there is not much dust on it. You never noticed it . . .'

'You did not notice it either, you were away only this morning. How is your sister?'

'I think you must have picked up the card and dropped it on the window sill without reading it . . .'

'Why didn't you read it, when you found it on the window sill . . . ?'

'I noticed it only after coming in now. Didn't he mention it?'

'I don't remember, he was talking so much.'

Finding them talking in whispers, Gopu got up and retired to his room.

Morning found them approaching the situation afresh. As soon as they were ready for the day, Gopu sat on the hall bench, subdued because of Sita's presence in the house. Nagaraj was still inaccessible, dressed in ochre and in the puja room, while Gopu sat silently fretting on the hall bench. As soon as Nagaraj was available Gopu asked, 'What do you propose to do? You expected to get an inspiration in the morning.'

'Morning hours are the best,' Nagaraj said, in order to keep the conversation at a safe level.

Gopu added a query and an answer. 'For what? For cleaning the cowshed?'

Nagaraj laughed with extra happiness, treating it as a joke and telling himself, 'This fellow will never forget cattle sheds and gobar gas even if he is placed in London,' and asked aloud, in continuation of his secret thought, 'Don't you ever wish to see London?'

Gopu was taken aback, but taking it casually as one of the irrelevancies to be expected from his brother, said, 'Yes, if Tim keeps vanishing like this.'

Another burst of laughter from Nagaraj, whose only aim was to maintain a cheerful atmosphere in order to convey an impression to Sita that all was well. Sita came out of the kitchen with relief in her face and asked, 'Will your brother want any special item for lunch?'

Gopu replied directly, 'Oh, Sita, don't bother about all that. Anything will do. My thoughts are on Tim. I must get him back and tell Charu, who has been moping and crying ever since we heard the news – '

'What news? Who is that busybody who tells you unnecessary things?' asked Nagaraj (without uttering a word).

Gopu pleaded, 'Sita, tell me what he said before leaving . . .'

'They left abruptly and there was not much speech. I was boiling water for the rice and when I heard his voice and turned around he was gone; even before I could ask him what was happening, he was gone with his wife. I ran to the door but he had arranged for an autorickshaw and was gone.' She had tears in her eyes when she added, 'I don't know what has upset them. I am praying and promising to the god in our temple to light a hundred wicks if he comes back safe.'

Nagaraj blurted out, 'There must have been more than one hundred wicks in the packet I brought you . . .'

Sita changed the subject immediately. 'You didn't ask for breakfast; have an early lunch?'

Nagaraj said, 'Should you ask? Have it ready. We will eat if we are feeling hungry. I always eat before going to the Boeing Centre, that saves a lot of labour for the lady . . .' in a jocular tone, 'But today I will stay back with you.'

Looking at Sita, who was fuming inside at her husband's way of speech, Gopu just said, 'I must first see the boy, wherever he may be. Other things only later. I will go to Kismet. Where is it?'

'Oh, we can't go there,' said Nagaraj. 'They drink whisky and such things there. Don't worry that he is getting into bad habits – although he has eau-de-Cologne sprayed over his clothes sometimes!'

Gopu frowned and said, 'Eau-de-Cologne! What for? What is it?'

'It's a scent.'

Gopu ignored this as one of Nagaraj's habitual irrelevancies and said, 'He should not be there. I must go there immediately; where is it?'

'I have not been there at all, but I know it is in New Extension.'

'Come with me,' said Gopu peremptorily, and Nagaraj looked at his wife for help.

She said, 'Go and help your brother to bring him home.'

Nagaraj felt let down by his wife, and said weakly, 'I have never been there. I don't know anyone there.'

Gopu looked at him and said in a firm tone, 'You are going with me.'

Nagaraj said, rubbing his chin, 'I have not had a shave today . . .' and threw an apprehensive look at his brother's unshaven state. Gopu was not in a mood to continue the talk. Nagaraj looked at Sita to see if she might have second thoughts and help him out. She looked away, and Nagaraj thought, 'Lady Macbeth! You want your husband to be damned. But Shakespeare has nowhere indicated that Macbeth had to go to a tavern . . .'

Gopu got busy to leave. He went in and came out a moment later wearing his grey coat buttoned up to his neck. He hustled Nagaraj, who pleaded, 'I am hungry, aren't you?'

'Sita, give him a glass of buttermilk. I can't wait.'

Nagaraj appealed, 'Let us go after the meal.'

'Yes, food will be ready soon. It will be better to eat before starting out,' added Sita, 'as you may not know when you will be back.'

After food, Nagaraj had no choice but to go in and groom himself as best as he could before his mirror. He then started out with his brother, looking back at Sita standing at the street door with a last hope that she would pull him back. She was cold and firm and advised Nagaraj in an undertone, 'Tell that poor girl that we miss her music.'

'Impossible,' Nagaraj thought. 'That means no Narada ever . . .'

They went down Kabir Street to Market Road, where an autorickshaw could be found, Nagaraj dreading his brother's propensity to haggle and quarrel with the driver over the fare. He said to his brother, 'All the auto-drivers are my friends. Let me pay the fare.'

Gopu did not pay any attention to his suggestion but walked down Market Road in grim silence, looking straight ahead. He seemed determined to walk to New Extension. Nagaraj said, 'It's far off, beyond the level crossing.'

'Do you know how much I trudge in the fields every morning?'

'Must be a lot . . .'

'We have to walk to the next village sometimes.'

'Sturdy fellow!' Nagaraj said. 'But here in the town . . .' he began.

Gopu did not encourage him to continue his sentence, but said, 'When I meet Tim and talk to him, you don't talk.'

'Why?' asked Nagaraj.

'It is so.'

'You could have left me behind. I told you I would wait for you at home . . .' Nagaraj ventured to say.

'Ask someone where is this Kismet.'

There was a passer-by whom Nagaraj accosted. He did not know, much to Gopu's annoyance. Gopu ordered, 'Ask someone intelligent. This man looks a ragamuffin.'

'Why can't you do it yourself? Am I your slave or lackey?' asked Nagaraj inwardly. But he said out loud suddenly, 'We should ask Tim himself! Ah, there he is!'

Gopu could not believe his eyes. There he was: Tim, carrying a shopping bag. He didn't see them, was about to turn into a lane. Both the brothers were overwhelmed at the sight of him and shouted, 'Tim! Tim!' Tim turned round, looked at them on the corner, and it was his turn to disbelieve his eyes. He stared at them and stopped. The meeting was emotional. Gopu's cheeks were wet with tears. Nagaraj found himself tongue-tied. Gopu said, 'You live here?' looking around at the narrow lane, littered with rubbish in a colony of thatched huts. Tim gave no direct reply. He led them to a stone bench in a corner and made them sit on it.

'Where do you live?' the brothers asked.

Tim flourished his arm to indicate a direction and asked, 'Why did you come here?'

The brothers answered simultaneously, 'To call you back home.'

'I am not coming,' said Tim, hugging his shopping bag.

Gopu was speechless with rage and disappointment and said, 'I am not going back without you.'

Tim ignored the challenge.

'Where is Saroja?'

'In the house.'

'She is keeping well?'

'How is her harmonium?'

Nagaraj wanted to say, 'If you live in a hut, a harmonium must sound terrible in the narrow space.' But Nagaraj remembered his brother's order not to talk. Still, he managed to say, 'We miss you both. Sita wants Saroja back urgently . . .'

'Why?' asked Tim, and did not wait for an answer. He suddenly turned away from them.

Gopu said, 'We want to see Saroja.'

'She has gone out.'

'Where?'

No answer.

'We wish to visit your home . . .'

'It is far off . . .'

'But you said it was here . . .'

No answer.

Tim suddenly left them sitting on the stone bench. The brothers stared at each other, not knowing what to make of it. After waiting and watching the direction in which he went, Gopu said to Nagaraj, 'Stay here, I will find out where he lives.' He followed in the direction in which Tim had gone. Nagaraj sat there brooding. Tim seemed to look well. Then why worry? There were instances in the history of mankind where people walked out suddenly, like Buddha, and became famous, actually doing better than those who stuck to home and followed the conventions. Tim would some day emerge as a world philosopher or leader. Till then, would he be living in one of the hovels? Was it necessary? He could live in Kabir Street and become great. But he remembered with regret that no world figure or even local leader ever came from his street; he remembered that when Mahatma Gandhi passed this way, they could not find anyone to offer him flowers from Kabir Street. Not even a trace of one great personality in a hundred years. But probably Saroja would become a famous singer with her harmonium. Horrible instrument. But for some mysterious reason people seemed to favour it. Why think of people? At home Sita herself seemed to enjoy the harmonium noise, having been a player when he had gone to inspect her, his future bride, years ago. His mother put an end to it. Good mother! What is to happen to Narada in this jungle of harmonium lovers? He stopped thinking, and asked, 'Where is this Kismet? No sign of it anywhere . . .' Was it fictitious? But the Talkative Man seemed to be a regular visitor there. Bachelor and moneyed, and no one to question even if he got drunk every day . . . He sensed a foul smell around and noticed a garbage mound at his back being rummaged by crows and hens. 'Where is Gopu? How long should I wait in this stench?' Thoughtless of Gopu to leave like this. But why blame him while he himself didn't possess enough sense to resist him?

Nagaraj was stuck there much like Casabianca on the deck of the burning ship (Nagaraj's literary allusions floating up from the depths of his subliminal self). He sat on the stone bench attempting to swat the flies attacking him from the garbage pile, and felt choked with the stench. A young goatherd stood in front of him, staring, while his animal was nosing in the rubbish heap. Nagaraj felt annoyed. 'Go away, what's your business here?' he said commandingly, surprised at the tone he had assumed. The boy moved off obediently. Nagaraj cried, 'Hey, what about your animal?' The boy ignored his question and hurried away. 'That goat may not be his, or may find its way home,' he reflected.

The sun was scorching. 'Not an inch of shade anywhere . . . Horrible place, never suspected Malgudi could be so bad. Must talk to someone. Chakravarthi, the Municipal Chairman, is lazy and indifferent; also I don't know him at all, and even if I came face to face with him I wouldn't be able to attack him, so what is the use of complaining? But whatever may be the reason, it's his business to see that garbage doesn't develop into a hillock anywhere. But what can anyone do? Quite a lot of junglees have invaded the town, attracted by the promise of work on the new railway line to Mempi. Too much of a dream; they will not take it up in this generation, although ministers make speeches.'

He felt hungry, had never strayed so far away from the Boardless at tiffin time. He guessed that the time must be three in the afternoon, judging from the slant of the western sun. 'What does Gopu mean by leaving me like this? He thinks he can do what he pleases with me, just an order, "Stay here," and I obey like a fool. How long? Till the end of Time when the sun would be extinguished and deluge and darkness overtake the universe, as in the chapters of *Narad Puran*.' And he wouldn't know his way back, and what was to happen to Sita? 'She'd become a petrified statue in Kabir Street.' He shuddered at this vision.

An old man who was passing along stopped to ask, 'Are you in pain?'

Nagaraj smiled and said, 'No, but I heard some noise, must be a strange bird flying low.'

The old man lingered, seemed willing to talk, and Nagaraj felt kindly towards him and asked, 'Where do you live?'

'At the level crossing; they have given me a small shed, and when the train passes I warn people and hold a flag. Even then people get run over sometimes. What can I do? Before the signal comes up people want to dash across and reach the other side in a hurry . . . Oh, after that the crowd and police and the wailing of relatives! . . . I am sick of this life. I have served the railway for thirty years. I was a porter at the station at one time and no worry there.' He was talking and also walking away.

Nagaraj watched him go though he wanted to enquire about Kismet. He let him go. 'I wish he had stopped to talk to me. But everyone is in a hurry and passing on. I am stationary like a milestone. The procession passes. Why can't I also pass instead of being a milestone? People take advantage of my milestone nature. Gopu called me "idiot" this morning, or was it yesterday? I can't remember; this blazing sun is melting my brain and memory. Gopu was right. If I am not an idiot, who else could be one? Gopu has a genius for coining phrases, "unleashed donkey" is his term and Tim has proved so, otherwise why would he be carrying a shopping bag in this garbage colony? If we had at least stopped to utter a word of explanation, we could have stuck to him and not let him off so easily. Gopu has messed it up by following him, leaving me behind. How long should I wait here? He has condemned me to live in this stench, and I am powerless to move. I think he casts a spell on an idiot – must have practised it at his gobar gas farm. Villagers would be up to anything. Otherwise why can't I use my head and rise and walk off? I fear him. If he comes back and doesn't find me, he'll blow up in anger or miss his way home? Laughable; even before I did, he knew this town and loafed around all day with his friends, driving me off from his company, and Father used to thrash him from time to time. I was not considered fit for their company. Phew! What a notion! I have survived and they have vanished into thin air. Probably his gang is still there, but fat and old and unrecognisable, and secretly in touch with Gopu in the village, spying on me and Tim all the time. Gopu constantly brags, "I know what's going on here. I have my own sources . . ." He means all his toothless, bald friends who have no better business than to spy, crafty beggars!'

Far off a train whistled. Nagaraj thought of the level crossing watchman and hoped he would have reached his post in good time. 'I forgot to enquire what he was doing here in this stinking place instead of minding the crossing. Must have gone to visit a friend or relative. In his absence who would mind the railway crossing? No wonder people get run over. At this rate he will be responsible for reducing the population of this town, which is already getting crowded with jungle folk. Jungle folk should remain in jungles, otherwise they will get run over at level crossings. Ultimately the authorities will put up gates at the crossing to save the lives of men, not to speak of cattle; it's a sin to kill a cow, so they say in all our shastras, and yet we don't protect them. They must put up a gate soon . . .'

He would tell the Talkative Man to write about it to the newspapers. 'What is a journalist for unless he acts as the mouthpiece of the community? Ministers will promise, and we may get it, as well as the Mempi Railway, at the end of Kaliyuga, when a new Avatar of Vishnu called Kalki is expected, riding on a white horse and wielding a blazing sword. "When virtue disappears and evil flourishes, I'll come and destroy the world," has promised God in the Gita.' He paused to verify if he was quoting the scripture correctly, but was not sure. 'Is this the place to recite the scriptures?' Amidst this rubbish and pigs, which he noticed were now rummaging the garbage where the goat had left off a little while ago. 'Why should I stay in these surroundings? – one who has belonged for generations to a Kabir Street family, honoured and respected. Gopu is responsible for reducing me to this wretched state.' He felt furious at this thought and briskly got up, muttering, 'Let him blow up when he comes back. If he can't find his way home, let him stay where he pleases – will serve him right . . . "Am I my brother's keeper?" asked Cain, and Gopu is Cain, he has almost killed me . . .'

He got up resolutely and retraced his steps. 'I was a fool not to have thought of it earlier.' It was tiring, and he had to trudge for nearly one hour before he could reach his familiar world of Market Road east. He looked at Bari's as if he had been lost to this world, and felt reassured. He resisted the impulse to enter Bari's and speak to him of Narada. He had missed his lessons for several days now. There were still five books of notes untouched, thanks to Saroja's harmonium and Tim's walk-out, so he could let Bari alone for a considerable time. Would it not be proper to inform him? He might conclude that Narada was dropped. He thought of arresting his step and shouting into the shop, 'I am still at it, don't imagine I am giving up Narada. As long as I live . . .' The meeting might not end in such a businesslike manner. Bari would invite him in to see some new stock of this and that and talk of Hamilton Bond, and chase Sunil up the ladder or out to fetch tea. All that would take time. He was hungry. First things first. He hurried on to the Boardless. Varma welcomed him, and Nagaraj had a feeling of being restored to civilisation after having been abducted by some demon and confined in hell.

Varma, sitting on his throne-like seat at the cash table, asked, 'What has happened to you? I have not seen you for three days.'

Nagaraj wondered for a moment how to explain. 'Oh, home duties. My wife was away to see her sister from Ceylon, and with a daughter-in-law in the house . . .'

'Oh, I didn't know you had a grown-up son.'

'Not exactly, but almost one. I am fond of him . . .' He fumbled on, afraid that he might utter some compromising statement about Tim and his Kismet. He knew Varma held strong views on Kismet but he had a short memory. 'Thank God he doesn't remember Tim, though he has seen him on several occasions.' Varma was muddled enough not to remember anyone among the scores of patrons coming in every day.

Nagaraj thought it best to change the subject. 'From Ceylon my sister's wife has brought cloves, dark and pungent; we don't see such cloves here. Only insipid stuff in our shops.'

'You are right; they extract oil and market only the chaff. For my sweets, I get them directly from Kabul or somewhere: dark ones, thick and oily . . .'

Nagaraj ordered tiffin and coffee and moved to a corner table where he could eat in peace. He noticed the Talkative Man come in and take his seat on a special chair beside Varma's throne, as had been the custom from time immemorial. When he noticed Nagaraj, T.M. came over and joined him. Drinking his coffee he said, 'Nag, I was busy the whole day with your brother.'

'Where is he?'

'Well, it's a long story . . .'

Nagaraj had to get it off his chest, could not contain himself. 'Fool of a fellow, he made me wait at a stinking place and never turned up. Where is he?'

'Gone back.'

'Home?'

'Yes, to his village.'

Nagaraj said, 'Strange man, to keep me waiting and go away without telling me!'

'Listen to me, let me finish my coffee first and then we will talk in a quiet corner. Too much babble and noise around here.'

They left after coffee. Nagaraj was unable to contain his curiosity. They walked down Market Road towards Ellaman Street. Nagaraj felt he was being teased by the other. He reflected as they walked along, 'Why should I show any interest? I don't care what has happened to a fellow who cast me on the rubbish dump and made me starve under the hot sun . . .'

The Talkative Man said, 'I've to peep in at a house in Ellaman Lane and take some notes and then I am free to talk to you.'

Nagaraj's curiosity was aroused and he asked, 'What, notes for your newspaper?'

'Nag, yes, this man claims to be able to stand on his head continuously for seventy-two hours without food and wants to get into the Guinness Book.'

'What is that?' Nagaraj asked, saying to himself, 'I don't care whatever it is; if you do not tell me in a few words about Gopu, I will turn round and go home. I am not keen on your company at the moment . . .' The Talkative Man was elaborating on the subject of the Guinness Book, all of which fell on deaf ears.

'You must tell me in six words what has happened instead of keeping me on tenterhooks. I am not interested if someone stands upside-down for a whole lifetime. In a sense, most people manage their lives upside-down: Trisanku inherited a whole heaven which was upside-down, himself permanently suspended at this angle through eternity. But where was Narada when all this happened?'

'How thoughtful you have become these days!'

'Oh, I have to think of – '

'Mostly about Tim, I am sure.'

'How did you guess?'

'One doesn't need to guess; your mind is an open book.'

'You are mistaken, my boy, while I'm myself not sure where my thoughts go,' thought Nagaraj, and decided to conceal the subject uppermost in his mind. He remained glum and silent while T.M. dashed into a house on the way, leaving him standing under a street lamp. 'Today,' reflected Nagaraj, waiting, 'everyone seems to plan to sentence me to wait. Thank God there is no garbage here; fairly clean, only a little cow dung here and there, which might appeal to Gopu – he might love to take it home to his village and feed the gobar gas plant . . .' He trembled at the thought of Gopu, in suspense of what might be in store when T.M. would speak. Perverse fellow: if he had said whatever it might be over their coffee, where they had all the time, which he spent in local gossip about sales tax corruptions . . .

Till they reached the river steps and sat down with their feet in the cool river, T.M. avoided the subject, and then began, 'You are dying, I know, to hear about Gopu. I'll tell you only this. He has gone back.'

'Where?'

'To his village home. He went straight to the bus stand.'

'But his bag is in my house. Hasn't he taken it?'

'No. The bus stand was nearby and he left.'

Nagaraj thought, 'You are known as the Talkative Man, but you don't know how to begin and carry on the story.' But he said aloud, 'How do you know that he has left?'

'Because he stuck to me the whole day. Till I saw him off I could not attend to any other work.'

'He left me sitting alone and then stuck to you? It is absurd. Didn't even take leave of me.'

'How could he, while you were so far away? Don't you want to know how I was caught up?'

Nagaraj, for some obscure reason, wanted to seem indifferent, while longing to cry out, 'Oh, tell me, tell me everything – don't delay.'

'I felt a little shocked when I saw him in New Extension, a more incongruous fixture one cannot imagine in that background. I could not recognise him in this setting of villas and avenues, having seen him only in your company in Kabir Street. Moreover, I never had much to do with him. That type of village elder usually puts me off. At the turning of New Extension main street, he was going and he spotted me before I spotted him, otherwise it would have been a different story. I was riding my bicycle and passed him as he came up, wearing his grey coat, striding along resolutely with the look of a man out to smash something. There was a fierce glint in his eye. I didn't recognise him but said to myself, "Here is a man I would never like to collide with." His face was covered with perspiration. He was swinging his arms like an athlete.'

Nagaraj said, 'He started out without a shave.'

'Yes. I noticed the stubble and his pink-edged dhoti, and took my bicycle off in a wide detour – you know why?'

'In order to avoid him.'

'Ah, you have understanding!' cried T.M. appreciatively. 'You are right, I didn't want to meet him; some instinct, I suppose!'

'Still he has not told me anything,' Nagaraj thought with some irritation. 'Let him go on like this a whole year by this river, and I am not going to ask, "What happened? Why did he leave me baking in the sun beside that rubbish dump on a hot stone?"' Indulging in such private thoughts, he missed some of the connecting sentences that the other had been uttering. He had also spent some moments enjoying the rumble of the river; the low splash and swish and the far-off strains of rough music from cartmen crossing Nallappa's grove while urging their animals on, the sounds softened by the distance. He thought, 'Birds are just starting to come back to the trees,' while the Talkative Man was concluding, 'And so I had to resign myself to the inevitable and set aside all my plans for the day and guide him to Kismet. After all, I said to myself, he is an old family friend, though he looks tough. But he would not leave, holding on to the handle of my bicycle; he looked mad, I tell you.

His eyes were bloodshot from walking in the sun. Was he starving?'

'Oh no, Sita insisted upon feeding us before we left.'

'But he looked fatigued.'

'So was I, waiting for him . . . Serves him right,' added Nagaraj.

T.M. said, 'Listen, don't interrupt me. I lose the thread . . .'

'And also the needle?' Nagaraj asked soundlessly, and laughed within at the quip.

'He created a scene at the door of Kismet. The sentry would not allow him to enter because of a dress regulation in that club – no one clad in a dhoti is permitted to enter the hall. Your brother was just wearing a rough dhoti and his grey coat, and he challenged the sentry. "You are descended from which heaven? Are you all Europeans here?" I tried to intervene, "There is a bye-law, we will change it soon, till then . . ." "I don't care," he cried. "I must see my son who is held here. I'll inform the police . . . ! You can't stop me. I won't go without him!"

'"There is no one inside at this hour." "Where is he?" he cried, "You are lying, you have hidden him here! I won't go till I see him. Do what you like . . ." He sat down cross-legged right in the middle of the entrance. 'You produce my son, or let me in to seek him out . . ." I was respected in the club, where I have been a member since it opened. I regretted I ever showed him the way.'

'Do you drink whisky all day?' Nagaraj wished to know, picturing him in that background, lounging and dissipating. 'No wonder you are hardly to be seen . . .' But aloud, 'Every day! All the time! You must be busy, very busy . . .'

'Indeed I am. I have a corner where I do my reports after news-hunting in the city, before going on to the railway station to despatch the letter. I also meet a lot of people there . . .'

'And more whisky then?' Nagaraj thought, but said, 'You have an interesting life.'

'That we will discuss later. Now, about your brother. While

he sat there no one could pass in without jumping over him. The Secretary arrived and asked, "Why are you here? Who are you?" "I have come to take my son, Krishnaji, and they won't let me in . . ." The Secretary looked at his dress and unshaven face, and decided that he was dealing with a crazy visitor, and was guarded. He threw a look at me and I nodded. He whispered to the watchman, who went in and brought a chair and placed it in a corner of the verandah, and said to Gopu, "Go and sit in that chair, sir, you should not obstruct . . ."

'"Where is my son?" Gopu demanded without budging.

'"Take that chair, he'll come."

'"No, I don't want any chair. I want to go in and search."

'The Secretary was irritated and said, "Only members are allowed in . . ."

'"Is my son a member? If so, what does he do?"

'"I'm not here to answer your questions. You please go, otherwise . . ." I knew what he meant. There was a strongman on the staff at the bar who had to persuade or push out troublesome customers. I had been passive and quiet, but at this point I beckoned to the Secretary and whispered, "Be kind to him, he is a respectable man; let us be tactful."

'"He must leave before members start coming. Can't be blocking the way . . ."

'I said, "I'll take him in as my guest."

'"Till we change the bye-laws about dress . . ." he began. The Secretary was a funny man, always concerned with bye-laws and daily complaining that the President was too slow and indifferent and would not convene the committee. While he was being eloquent on the subject, I had to keep telling him, "We must do something about that man." Gopu watched us like a bear in a trap. Also I remembered he used to picket liquor shops and stores selling foreign cloth by lying across the doorway in those days when young men joined the satyagraha movement started by Mahatma Gandhi. They called in the strongman when they found Gopu adamant.

When the strongman tried to lift him, Gopu proved a match for him. All the peasant strength in him came to the surface. "Keep your hands off. Don't touch me, you fool!" he cried. The strongman was nonplussed, and stood still. The Secretary said, "Take him out, I am ordering you." Members started coming in. They stood about for a moment watching him and passed in, jumping over him to reach the card tables or the bar without waste of time. A man scowled at the obstruction and demanded of the Secretary, "What is this? Who is he? Why don't you clear the way? How do you expect us to get in?"

'Gopu just repeated, "I have come to take away my son."

'The Secretary said, 'He has not come yet."

'"You are lying, hiding him; I know he must be inside," said Gopu. Some members stood around in groups. The Secretary told the strongman, "Take this man off the door and put him down in that chair, and keep him there." The strongman, used to obeying only such specific orders, bent down and encircled his arms around Gopu as a preliminary to heaving him up. Gopu shrieked in his ear, "I have told you not to touch me; get away, you fool!" I did not know what to do, so moved away and hid myself behind a pillar. The Secretary repeated to the strongman, "Take him, I say, don't you hear me? What are you waiting for, you fool?" The strongman wailed, "He is like a stone. Can't shake him . . . !"

'"Take him, I say, and throw him out." At this, the strongman tried a stranglehold grip on Gopu; now Gopu disentangled his hand and hit the strongman in the face so hard that the strongman reeled back, and when he recovered and came on again with a war cry, determined to maintain his reputation, Gopu just flicked him off, and the strongman tottered back and fell off the verandah into a flowerbed below. When he picked himself up and tried to make another attempt, I said to him softly, "Don't. He may kill you." The strongman accepted my advice and retreated, somewhat bruised in mind and body. I felt proud of Gopu. Never knew a Kabir Street fellow-being could be so strong.'

'Was my brother hurt?' Nagaraj asked solicitously.

'Far from it,' said the T.M. 'The strongman was the one who was demolished. I am sure he will lose his job, being employed chiefly for clearing the club of members who refuse to leave after closing time. Now Gopu seemed to have damaged his reputation. Gopu sat tight, repeating like a mantra, "Give me back my son . . ." A circle formed around him of some men who were pleading with him to rise and go to the chair and wait for his son. Members were discreet enough not to go too near him. Someone was asking, "Who is his son?"

'"That young fellow who works here, and his wife is the one who plays the harmonium and sings in the evenings."'

'Even here!' reflected Nagaraj.

'"Send for him at once," ordered the President of the club.

'"He has already arrived and slipped in by the other door."

'"Call him!"

'"He refuses to come out!"

'"Tell him his father is waiting, creating a scene . . ."

'"We have told him!" The end of it was that Tim refused to meet his father. When Gopu learnt that Tim would not recognise him, he rose to his feet, much to everyone's relief. I was afraid he might dash in and bite someone, but he only stood at the door for a moment, looked for me in the crowd and nodded, then turned and went down the steps. I joined him at the gate. He said, "Take me to the bus stand, I am going back."

'"To Kabir Street?"

'"No, to my village."

'I led him to the bus stand. He got into his bus without a word.'

'Did he not want to take his jute bag which he has left behind?' asked Nagaraj, inanely.

CHAPTER 15

A week passed. Sita went on grumbling about the incident, and the indignity suffered by Gopu, for which she somehow held Nagaraj responsible. She kept saying, 'You should not have left him alone.' Nagaraj thought, 'This woman will not understand my position. No use my repeating that he had asked me to wait for him. Perhaps she doesn't believe my word; she doesn't want to. All the blame on me!'

Nagaraj received a postcard from Gopu, with the message: *I have no son. I disown him. You have misappropriated and ruined him completely. You may adopt him and assign your property to him as your successor so that you may have someone who will have the right to ignite the funeral pyre when you die . . . being as you are without an issue even after so many years of married life and I know how you have steadily worked to achieve this purpose all your life, plucking him away from me and Charu when he was only two months old.*

Nagaraj was agitated when he read the card; he resolved to suppress it and not let Sita see it. But she had been the one to receive it from the postman when Nagaraj was away at the Boeing Centre. She shed tears when she read it, but simply dropped it on the window sill and did not refer to it when Nagaraj came home, leaving it to him to discover it.

Nagaraj felt choked while picturing himself on the funeral

pyre with Tim as his successor applying the burning faggot, according to the rules, in order to ensure a smooth passage to heaven. He suddenly felt touched by Gopu's solicitude to send him heavenward smoothly, where probably material for Narada would be more directly accessible, or even the sage himself might materialise and guide him. Death has its good points. But a son at the firing point was essential; after all, Gopu's suggestion for adoption might be well intentioned, though crude-sounding. Nagaraj thought he should find out more about the process of adoption. Might not be a bad idea, after all. He decided to discuss it with Sita at an appropriate time. He must consult the old family priest first. Whenever it might happen, he was going to ask to be sent upward in his ochre robes, which had all along prepared him for his final journey in small daily doses . . .

He thought of Sita in this connection, widowed and forlorn after being inseparable from him for thirty or forty years, and was filled with pity for her, all alone in this vast house. But she would have Tim as her adopted son, and the harmonium-playing daughter-in-law (through adoption, of course). In any case there was not likely to be any objection or trouble, and she herself loved that horrible instrument. Saroja could tote it around the whole house, sit down anywhere she liked and release the cacophony. He would not be there to hear and suffer, unless he came back as a ghost. Would he have to haunt Kabir Street? He felt somewhat lighter and pleasant while viewing himself as a ghost, but the picture of his body on the funeral pyre, with Sita bewildered and crushed, overwhelmed him with self-pity and tears streamed down his cheeks, and he was convulsed with an involuntary sob just at the moment when Sita came up to the pyol. She observed his state, took his hand and suggested, 'Let us go in. People are watching; I see the engineer from the last house coming . . . Let us go in quick.' She led him in to the hall bench. They sat there for a while in silence. She said, controlling the tremor in her voice, 'You must not take it to heart. Your brother has always been somewhat rough with you, but he means no harm; he must be upset with Tim. But what can anyone do with him? I think your brother must be feeling it more keenly for Charu's sake; after all, she is the mother and wants her son. What can anyone do with Tim? He cannot be influenced. Don't bother about his postcard, he has written it in a bad mood. At Kismet Tim should have come out to see him . . .'

For a few days a terrible gloom. Nagaraj felt it acutely. 'It is better to have loved and lost than never to have loved at all,' he kept repeating irrelevantly, another quotation sticking out in some corner of his mind. 'Where is it from?' he speculated constantly. 'Shakespeare? Of course, source of ninety per cent of the world's wealth of quotations, no – ninety-nine per cent. The balance of one per cent shared by the Bible, Koran, Bhagavad Gita, and Palgrave's Golden Treasury.' He felt proud that he was familiar with such literary treasures. How? He was a little confounded since he had no memory of any regular studies; whatever he remembered was from cursory, casual browsing. Mostly at the Town Hall library in the early days when he regularly visited the library, actually hanging around the place from morning till evening in the days of the benign old librarian, who allowed him a lot of freedom to pull out a volume from any shelf. More than anything, he let him rummage among book dumps left there by neighbouring families who wanted to clear the space in their homes. There in the dumps were a miscellany of publications, from outdated catalogues and law reports to world classics in tatters. Nagaraj spent much time squatting beside the dump in an antechamber, browsing. Recollecting, he felt he had gathered a jumble of literary tit-bits, and most of them had sunk deep in his mind and floated up at unexpected, irrelevant moments. He was filled with self-admiration, but realised that he could not have continued this practice: the old librarian retired and a hot-headed youngster took his place. Nagaraj remembered with some bitterness how brusquely he had dismissed the study of Narada. 'Also, I must say in fairness to everyone, after the Boeing Sari Centre came into being, I had no time for library visits.' He chuckled within himself as he thought of his brother Gopu, who had no doubt passed B.A. – God knows by what miracle! – but an ignoramus, boor, and writer of offensive postcards and one who had made himself ridiculous at Kismet. All that he cared for was his gobar gas plant; that was his university and library combined. He had a good memory and could mug up his textbooks and pass, that was all. Did he know a single quotation from anywhere? He chuckled again. At this moment Sita came out and noticed his elation. 'Sita, don't you agree that Gopu is an ignoramus?'

'He is a B.A.,' she said.

'So am I,' said Nagaraj.

'Why think of it now?' she asked. 'It was so long ago.'

'Wonder how he passed? Must have bribed the professors,' he said mischievously.

'Why don't you think of something else? Always obsessed with your brother . . .'

'But do you think he remembers Shakespeare?'

'Think of something else,' she said and went in.

Nagaraj reflected, 'She is a good girl, won't make things worse by agreeing with me. Good girl, Sita. So is Charu, Gopu's wife, though somewhat haughty. Am I right? No, why should I call her haughty? Unreasonable thought. My anger with Gopu is reflected on her; unfair. One may say the worst things of him and be right, still fall short of the full description. He is like one of those asuras in the puranas, headstrong and haughty and vile. But in every case they had a downfall, if not destroyed totally. Evil destroys itself, say our scriptures. How will Gopu's downfall come?' He gloated over this prospect for a while. 'Maybe by some catastrophe such as a thunderbolt hitting his gobar gas plant, or through an obstinate pest attacking his farm or a poisonous seed spreading amongst his grass, laying prostrate his cattle. With his hundreds of coconut, banana, mango and guava trees gone, and his farmhouse attached for unpaid taxes, he will be thrown out, and, carrying his bags, trudge all the distance from his village on foot, a bankrupt in rags with Charu hiding at his back, and knock on my door. What would be my first word of greeting? "Who are you, stranger? Your face is familiar!" Or should I say, "Begone, you hot-headed evil man. If you repent sincerely, you may step in and Sita will give you food . . ."'

After this day-dream he felt lighter at heart. He felt he had now got something of his own. One good deed Gopu had performed was to confound the Kismet gang and puncture the strongman. 'Going off to the bus without a word to us, not even taking back his jute bag. What did it contain?' Nagaraj felt an uncontrollable curiosity. He left his seat, softly went in, hesitated for a moment to be sure that the way was clear and that Sita was in the backyard, beyond the third court. Stepped in and shut the door of the middle room where Gopu had been staying. He found Gopu's jute bag kept in a corner. It had no lock and he quickly rummaged through its contents. He found a dhoti and a shirt and towel – only one change, apparently for another day's stay; he'd wash his daily set himself and put them out to dry. Nagaraj also found a rosary of sandalwood beads, a little well-thumbed book of morning prayers to address the sun, planets and the gods presiding therein, and all the sacred rivers, and the potent gayatri mantra, a little brass box containing sacred ash, and a packet of incense sticks. This was a revelation. Every morning after his bath Gopu shut himself in his room and prayed. He was not the kind to talk about it, but had a secret channel of communication with God, a private arrangement with eternity . . .

Nagaraj was overwhelmed by this idea and felt he had blasphemed a holy person by his wild, vicious thoughts. He begged pardon of the gods who, he felt, were aware of what was going on in his mind. He noticed a diary and felt tempted to open its pages and learn more of Gopu – if his prayers had any relevance to his daily life and human relationships, if he put on a porcupine exterior to cover an inner timidity . . . But he left the diary untouched as he had a feeling of being watched from the skies. At this moment, Sita called from outside, 'What are you doing?'

Nagaraj hurriedly packed the jute bag, shoved it in a corner and opened the door. Surprised, Sita asked, 'Why have you bolted the door?'

'I thought I might look through my notes for Narada here, quietly . . .'

'Afraid I would come and disturb?' she said rather petulantly, and added, 'I am not so foolish . . . But your notebooks are in the other room!'

'Yes,' Nagaraj said. 'That's why I am not looking through them now.' She could not accept his explanations and stood at the doorway staring at him. He found it disturbing and said with an apologetic grin, 'I can't deceive you. Your eyes pierce through me and see my soul. If I ever wanted to deceive you I had so many occasions, but I never tried it. You are a great wife for a man.'

She was rather amused by his rambling talk but stood firm as if she would get the truth out of him. She said, 'After all these years, you are talking as if we were newly-weds. What is it? Come out with it?'

He confessed.

She said, 'Oh, is that all? You and your brother! It's always that. You looked as if you were stealing someone's jewellery.'

'He is a careful man, won't carry valuables in his bag,' he said.

She lost interest in his enumeration of its contents and said off-tangent, 'Why don't you bring your notebooks to this room and write here, if you must, instead of in the other room?'

He resisted the idea.

She said, 'That room in the second courtyard is full of vermin and rats. Some day you will find all your notes on Narada completely eaten up and digested by the white ants which have covered the rafters, if you look up . . .'

'You have also mentioned rats,' Nagaraj said.

'Do you think I'm being funny? What the rats leave over in shreds will be finished off by white ants; they help each other . . .'

It seemed to him a good idea to move into this room for writing. He got busy at once. He strode up and down, carried a bundle of Crow-brand notebooks to the middle room table, adjusted the chair and arranged his Waterman's pen to be handy when inspiration seized him. He was satisfied when he looked around and felt that life's pendulum, which had swung erratically, was coming back to normal, which meant that in the background Narada would once again appear and lend a meaning to daily existence. Anyway, he told himself, it was all for the best. The house was now normal and quiet. No speculations about Tim. No need to watch his movements. No need to glorify and find excuses for the eau-de-Cologne smell. No need to hunt for earplugs. The house had become suddenly quiet; absolute calm prevailed. Sita too looked relieved and had shed her irritations and anxieties. Above all, he was free from responsibilities and custody of Tim. He could pray in peace and write in peace, sitting in a chair and at a table. He had never had the use of this table freely at any time. He threw his mind back. In their student days Gopu usurped the table and chair and drove him to a corner, where he had to crouch over a dealwood box and do his homework. When Gopu married, he shut himself in with Charu, chasing off Nagaraj to a corner in the hall. Later Tim, and still later Tim and Saroja and her harmonium occupied the room. Nagaraj felt he had somehow been kept off that table by fate. Now, for the first time, it was within his reach. He felt it was going to be a luxury for him to be able to place his notes on a table and write sitting in a chair. He had a fresh lease of life.

Next morning, after his prayers, he went straight to the pyol, throwing a word of cheer in Sita's direction. He hummed a little song, much to her amusement. She said, 'You have become suddenly young.'

'I have always been so. Only you didn't notice.'

'Maybe you don't need your ochre robe for writing.'

'No need. You will be the only one to talk, and I will answer. I can talk and write at the same time. Only I can't bear the harmonium noise.'

'Oh, that, and your brother! You can't get them out of your mind . . . Sometimes I feel I should play my harmonium again. My father spent fifty rupees a month for my tutor. I feel rather dull, I must say, without Tim and Saroja, and I dream sometimes I could resume my music . . .'

Nagaraj felt embarrassed. He thought, 'Why are these creatures music mad? Unfortunately, my opinion will provoke them.' He never expected Sita to have musical ambitions. He was at a loss for words to continue the conversation, but told himself, 'I must immediately secure cotton wool plugs, and depend on my ochre robe. I had thought I would not need them now.' He remained silent, and then said, 'I must begin my work tomorrow morning. Everything is ready – '

'Except the harmonium accompaniment,' she remarked with a grin.

He felt, 'She is still joking, will not take me seriously. First daughter-in-law and now the adopted mother-in-law! Women are an impediment. Ah, how could I say so? The deity of learning is Saraswathi, the goddess with a veena in one hand, and the book and other things in her four arms. I am condemning the whole race of women. Wrong, I think I am losing my head. Prolonged absence from Narada has affected my mind; I must get back to my work soon.'

He got up briskly from the pyol and went into his study, sat at his desk and browsed through his notes in the Crow-brand exercise book. He had filled up five books and it filled him with misgivings now. He had lost touch with the subject for some weeks, thanks to Tim's problems, and much of the notes seemed incomprehensible. He had lost touch with the origins of creation and all the darkness and gloom of Bari's book. Even after five notebooks had been filled there was no trace of the main character. Not even an ant seemed to have been created; still water, water everywhere. 'And not a drop to drink,' echoed a literary oddment from a corner of his vast store of jumbled memory. Today, re-reading his notes and his attempted composition based on them, he found that none of it made sense. He felt desperate, and cried out, 'Sita, come here!' The urgency in his voice made her anxious and she almost came down in a run from the second court, where she was leaning on a pillar and reading some magazine. 'What is it?'

Nagaraj pushed across the table a bundle of notebooks and said, 'If you need paper for lighting the oven, take these, take these away.'

She looked alarmed. Had never seen him in such a mood. She collected the books and held them to her bosom protectively. 'What has come over you?'

'They are useless. I think Bari has been foisting on me some nonsense, nothing to do with Narada.'

'Why don't you ask him really what that mysterious book is about? Ask him to read the later portions and see what comes.'

'Brilliant idea . . . I tried it but . . .'

'Ask him to dip into the old volume here and there to see if the sage is hiding anywhere . . .' And both laughed at this fantastic notion. This outburst relieved his mind and he reflected, 'Sita is not as bad as I think.' And at once he repented his secret thought. He touched his cheeks as was their habit while begging pardon for a mistake when young. Observing the motion of his hand, Sita asked, 'What excuse are you praying for and to whom?'

'Ah, how sharp you are! This man is lucky to have Sita for a wife.'

She blushed at this compliment and said, 'After so many years, you are discovering me. Thank Shiva. At least now you know me. But you have not answered my question, what excuse you were seeking from whom?'

'From God for not understanding you properly. I had thought you did not like Narada.'

'Still I don't understand your preoccupation with Narada.

Everyone knows that he was a great sage – that's all. No one has bothered to want to write his life story. Why should you alone bother?'

He had no answer; he blinked unhappily. He could only say, 'But others have written. Kavu pundit has four volumes in Sanskrit on the subject, and Bari has a big tome, which is over a hundred years old.'

'So why should you take the trouble again over the same subject?'

'So that our people may also know.'

'Why do you take upon yourself this task?'

'I don't know, I have always wanted to do it, felt it my duty somehow.'

She said coldly, 'You will be happier if you overcome it. It's only a notion which has somehow got nailed in your brain. Pluck out the nail. Nothing more; get rid of it.'

He listened in silence, echoing secretly Lady Macbeth's lines,

> I would, while it was smiling in my face,
> Have pluck'd my nipple from his boneless gums,
> And dash'd the brains out, had I so sworn
> As you have done to this.

'Sita's words sounded similar and had a flint-like sharpness, an inescapable logic and unambiguity, very much like Lady Macbeth's advice. She wants to remove Narada from the scene of action in a very Lady-Macbeth-like manner.' His heart bled at the thought of eliminating Narada, abandoning a personality who had occupied his thoughts all his waking hours for years. Sita noted his sudden silence and preoccupation and asked, 'You look suddenly sad. Why?'

He thought, 'Everyone wants my private thoughts and demands them to be exposed. After all, I too have a right to remain silent; if I speak out, no one can bear it. Out of consideration for others, and they assume I am a fool . . .' While these thoughts were racing along thus, she watched his face, and he just said, 'I am not . . .' and checked his sentence before 'fool'.

Sita watched his face with amusement and concluded, 'If you can't drop Narada, I've nothing to say. I only wanted to suggest you could write about God Krishna, his boyhood, childhood, and his championing of the Pandavas in the great battle . . . The subject is everywhere, easier than Narada.'

Nagaraj shook his head, 'What I want to write is something new, not widely known or appreciated. You will realise when it comes out . . .'

She withdrew suddenly, remembering something to do in the kitchen. Nagaraj stared after her for a while and said: 'She wants to avoid the subject, probably hates Narada. Nor will she accept these notes for fuel, which was a handsome offer on my part . . . but she picked up the notebooks and hugged them to her bosom. What does she mean? Difficult, women, difficult to understand. Whatever may happen, tomorrow I will start writing again at seven a.m. The times are propitious, no harmonium to madden me.' He suddenly shouted, 'Sita, tomorrow morning at seven o'clock I am going to continue my writing, even if the heavens fall. We will have to be up at five o'clock as usual, sorry to bother you, my dear.' He added within himself, 'This is a matter in which I alone can have a voice, not you, although in other matters you are welcome to speak your mind.' After this outburst, external and internal, he felt triumphant that he had established his standing not as one married to Sita but as the author of *Narad Maharaj*, as Bari would say. It was possible that the sage might reveal himself to him in a vision. Why not? Visions do not come by one's sweating for it, but unasked, as grace for concentrated meditation. 'I'll meditate on Narada more methodically hereafter.'

He rose with a new resolve and stretched his limbs, whispering to himself, 'You must never listen to women. They will not let you do anything worthwhile, nothing more important than buying brinjals and cucumber, and mustard and rice, and caressing whenever a chance occurred. One who is out to make a mark in any walk of life will have no chance.' His thoughts continued, 'What about my mother? Who knows how she must have nagged and reduced my father to what he became: just a grabber of village produce, bullying the cultivators who brought grains in cartloads. Even otherwise what would he have done, produced more than two brothers, perhaps? Ha! Ha! Wonderful brothers. A sister between us would have made some difference; she would have acted as a buffer. But poor Father had no time, having to brow-beat peasants from the village all the time and squeezing out their cash, while Mother kept providing him food hour by hour to satisfy his gluttony during the day and at night perhaps his carnal desires . . .

'Why am I thinking such thoughts of the poor man, who came every evening to the municipal school to take me home safely, although I wanted to play marbles in the street. How concerned he was when he took charge of my school books and carried them home; and then did my homework. I am an ungrateful wretch, indulging in evil thoughts. Poor Father, forgive me and don't send down any punishment from your seat in heaven. Forgive me, please. There is an evil half of me which floats to the surface at unexpected moments and provokes sinful thoughts. Please quell them. If you ever meet the great sage Narada in your heavenly home, please tell him to help and guide me in my effort, tomorrow morning at seven o'clock. Sita will be up at five. When I begin again there will be no stopping – all day I am going to write. I hope Bari is not deceiving me with a bogus Narada in his obscure volume; so far no sign of even that. However, tomorrow is D-Day, as they used to say during the war.'

At this moment, he heard a van stop in front of his house, and opened the door only to let in Tim, Saroja and the van driver who carried in, during several trips to and fro, two trunks, bedding rolls, a basket, a large-sized harmonium (which was known as a 'leg harmonium' and which had a stand, the bellows to be operated by a foot pedal leaving both hands free for the player to produce the maximum noise) and a folding chair. 'Got a good price for my old instrument and I was able to get this and the chair,' she explained to Sita who had come out and was watching the arrivals speechlessly. Nagaraj was confused, though he made several sounds of welcome and moved about between the street door and the middle room excitedly, accommodating and arranging their baggage, saying something all the time, not really knowing what to say. The persistent thought in his mind was, 'If you had brought ten pounds of cotton wool to plug my ears, it would not have sufficed, considering the monster you have brought in.'

Tim went to his room, looked around and at the table and said, 'These your books?'

Nagaraj picked them up apologetically. 'White ants and rats in that room – so Sita said . . .' He hurriedly took them to his bedroom and, unobtrusively, also his brother's jute bag. He wanted to add, 'I asked Sita to burn the notes but she clutched them to her bosom and put them back on your table . . .' But he only said aloud, 'I have not at all been able to write these days . . .'

'So busy?' asked the boy, sneeringly, as it seemed to Nagaraj.

'Not exactly, but I missed you . . . I am glad to see you . . .' He could not say anything more, nor ask why Tim had come back suddenly. He thought it best to avoid the question. Meanwhile Sita and Saroja were in the kitchen talking simultaneously and non-stop. Sita seemed to be particularly happy that Tim was back. She seemed to feel, 'Now our home is back to normal.' And Tim moved about the house as if nothing had happened or changed. Nagaraj had many questions to ask, but Tim gave him no chance. He shut himself in the room. Nagaraj had not the courage to knock on his door and enquire, ask, or investigate. 'He has come back in the same manner as he left – no explanation or any elaborate discussion – not in his nature, why should one expect anything different? I'll take him as he is. If his father wants him, he is welcome to come and take him. I am only a milestone. I stay and others come and pass. I must only watch, not ask questions. Tim's life and actions are, as ever, a mystery. But God has not endowed me with a temperament to solve mysteries. I have to accept them, that's all . . . I do not mind anything except that huge harmonium; when its bellows work, the roof will be lifted off the rafters and beams. I dread it. If I speak about it, they will both walk out again, and then Gopu will come down and badger me. I must be prepared for anything. If Tim walks out again, where will he go? Back to Kismet?'

This question was answered by Sita later that night in the privacy of their bedroom, after Tim had shut himself in with Saroja. Sita sat on the edge of Nagaraj's bed after closing the door and said in an undertone, 'Saroja said they have come to stay and are not going back to Kismet.'

'Why?'

'Because they belong to this house – and nowhere else to go.'

'Should we adopt him?' he wanted to ask but suppressed it, fearing that she might break down at the reminder of Gopu's postcard.

Sita added, 'Saroja said that Tim had a fight with the Secretary of Kismet, and described it with a lot of admiration for the way Tim waged it. She was earning fifty rupees an evening for singing and playing the harmonium for the members. It went on smoothly till they brought in the leg harmonium. The Secretary then came, while she was playing, to move her instrument to a side room, telling her to operate it there as it was too noisy and disturbed the club members who were assembled in the hall for playing cards or chatting. Tim dropped whatever he was doing at the moment, rushed up in a rage and shouted at the Secretary for insulting his wife. There was a lot of commotion while Tim pushed and slapped the Secretary. Saroja was afraid that they might call the police . . .'

'I wish the police had come and seized the harmonium,' Nagaraj said. 'I dread that tomorrow morning it will start blaring. I can have no hope of writing any more. You could as well take the notebooks back to the old room, where at least white ants may relish my notes on Narada . . . And another thing: don't be surprised if I wear the ochre robe when I am at home. It'll force me to remain silent and not speak out and upset the children and drive them out again. I shall also acquire a lot of cotton wool and try and pack it all in my ear so that even a thunderclap may sound like a whisper.'

Glossary

almirah – wardrobe, cupboard
asura – demon
banian – singlet
bonda – a sweetmeat
brinjal – aubergine, eggplant
dhoti – loincloth
jibba – tunic, robe
junglee – forest-dweller
jutka – two-wheeled vehicle drawn by horse
kama – lust
khaddar – handspun cloth
krodha – anger
lakh – one hundred thousand (rupees)
lobha – greed, avarice
moha – infatuation
puja – rights performed in Hindu worship
pundit – learned
purana – sacred legend of Hinduism
pyol – raised platform
rasam – beverage of spiced pepper-water
rishi – Hindu sage
sadhu – holy man
samadhi – profound meditation
sambhar – sauce of dal, vegetables and spices
sanyasi – holy man, dedicated to life of wandering mendicant
satyagraha – passive resistance
shastra – sacred Hindu law-book
veena – seven-stringed musical instrument